Trails
of the Soul

Karen D Hamilton

Trails of the Soul
Published by yes and also press, inc.
Centennial, CO

Publisher's Cataloging-in-Publication data

Names: Hamilton, Karen D., author.
Title: Trails of the soul / Karen D. Hamilton.
Description: Centennial, CO: Yes and also press, inc, 2021.
Identifiers: ISBN: 978-1-7341465-1-6
Subjects: LCSH Man-woman relationships. | Spirituality--Fiction. | Dude ranches--Fiction. | Love stories. | BISAC FICTION / Visionary & Metaphysical
Classification: LCC PS3608 .A684 T73 2021 | DDC 813.6--dc23

Cover art by Janet Hamilton

QUANTITY PURCHASES: Companies, professional groups, clubs, and other organizations may qualify for special terms when ordering quantities of this title. For information, email karen@yesandalsopress.com.

"It's only when you wake up out of the trauma and all its victimization mysteries and fears that you suddenly realize, 'Oh I see what all that is happening to me is about.'"

—William Brugh Joy

Chapter

1

"Hey, girl. Guess what? We're going on an adventure!"

Taryn had just walked into her condo, and was still sweaty from yoga class. When her phone rang, she was juggling her gear, so she'd grabbed her phone without looking to see who was calling. She'd had a hunch though that it was Paige, and instantly recognized the voice of her friend of nearly thirty years.

"Oh, hi. What are you talking about?"

"I went to that silent auction for the arts council last night. I had the winning bid on a week for two at a dude ranch. And you're coming with me!"

Taryn was perplexed, as she wrestled the towel out of her sports bag in frustration.

"A dude ranch? Are you kidding? Where? Why? Paige, I haven't been on a horse since I was a kid, and I know *I've* never seen you on a horse. What possessed you to bid on a dude ranch?"

"Well, it just sounded like fun. It's in Colorado; I forget the name of the town. Honestly I didn't expect to win it. But I did, and you have to come with me. Be good to get your mind off the date-that-shall-not-be-talked-about."

Taryn knew Paige was referring to the anniversary of her divorce, and she was right—it was not to be discussed. There had been so much talk in the months after—so much—that Taryn finally cut it off. The situation was unresolvable. No use hashing it out any more. She looked out her window at the lazy Seattle drizzle and sighed.

"Jeez, when? It's June already and I'm booked solid for the next two months."

"Yeah I know you better than that. You always leave the week after the big art show open. Which means you're free as a bird second week in September. Except now you're not. I already made the reservations. Done deal." Paige had a tone in her voice that told Taryn argument would be useless.

"Seriously, woman? I need time to wrap my head around this ... Let me call you back."

Taryn was exasperated. She and Paige had been friends since college, best friends, like sisters now really. And she was usually happy to go along with whatever off-the-wall schemes Paige came up with because they had such fun together. Especially since the breakup of her marriage to Wyatt. But a dude ranch? In God-knows-where Colorado?

She had to admit though—it was coming up on three years since the divorce and a distraction might be nice. Three years. It seemed like forever ago, and not, at the same time. In many ways the wounds were still fresh. The man she'd given her life to, twenty-three years' worth, suddenly up and has an affair with one of their friends, and leaves. It had taken her more than two years just to begin to get her bearings again, feel like she was physically present as a human being. Even now she didn't feel whole ...

Oh, my God, you have to stop thinking about this. Just call Paige and say yes, like you always do. Get the F away from here and have some fun.

"Paige? I'm in."

The last few weeks of summer were always a hectic flurry for Taryn. While she'd given up most of her work on the arts council after the divorce because too many of the friends she and Wyatt had shared were there, she still helped with the annual show in August. That was the time when she was especially glad she'd chosen to get the condo near downtown Seattle instead of keeping the house further north. She'd have burned up half the oil fields in Alaska traipsing back and forth to the gallery.

She also had to get her youngest, Amy, ready for her last year of college. It was gut-wrenching this time. They were so close. Because the divorce had been so difficult for Taryn, her daughter had continued to live with her for the first years of college. That time was ending now. Amy had interned during the summer for a graphics design company just north of Seattle. She really wanted to work for them after graduation, and they'd already offered her a job. As she would be moving into an apartment with two of her college friends, she wouldn't be returning home again. Since Taryn's older son Josh had moved on too, she was facing the empty nest phase of her life. As proud as she was her little ones were ready to take their places as adults, she was not particularly looking forward to it. She'd already lost her "wife" identity and now "mother" would go too. Leaving her with ... she had no idea.

The day the movers were coming for Amy's things, Taryn took her to lunch at her daughter's favorite rooftop restaurant. The hostess sat them at a table with a great view, and Taryn breathed in slowly as she ran her eyes over the city she loved. Amy caught her mother's gaze and drank in the sights too, until the waiter arrived. They ordered quickly. As many times as they'd come to this place, both had their favorites already in mind—dill salmon and a spinach salad for Taryn, black and blue burger with sweet potato fries for Amy.

"So, here we are. The end of your childhood, so to speak. Think you're ready to take on the world?" Taryn's eyes got moist and she looked quickly at the skyline to regain some composure.

"I am, Mom. You taught me well. Senior year's gonna be fun, but I'm already looking forward to getting to work at McKinley Johnson & Chapman." She cocked her head to one side and peered at her mom. "And I'll bet you're going to enjoy having the condo all to yourself."

"Well, it will be nice not to have your books strewn about everywhere—I'll admit that," Taryn said with a smile. "But I'm going to miss you horribly. You, and Josh too, are my best friends and I've loved being able to talk to you every day. It's going to be so different now. Phone conversations just aren't the same." Taryn pouted. "How are we going to hug over the phone?"

"Mom, I'm not moving all that far away. We'll get together lots, I promise." Amy reached out to touch Taryn's hand. "And I hear you have something fun coming up with Paige. A dude ranch is it?"

"Oh good grief. I still can't believe I let her talk me into that one. I mean, really." She shook her head and took a sip of the sparkling water the waiter had just delivered.

"Mom, you're going to have a blast. You always do when Paige drags you off on one of her excursions."

Taryn winced. "Actually Amy, there's something about this one that has me a bit nervous. I just have this unsettling feeling that the week will shake up my life in some way."

Amy raised her hands palm up in a "huh?" gesture. "Like how? It's a dude ranch. Barring some freak accident involving falling off a horse—don't do that by the way—how could that be?"

"I don't know. It doesn't make sense, but I'm kind of on edge about it for some reason." Taryn grimaced, then brightened. "Enough of that. I talked to Josh yesterday, and he said you've changed some of the classes you were going to take this semester. Tell me about them."

They'd nearly finished their meal when Taryn glanced at her watch. "Oh, heavens, look at the time. We need to get back—the movers will get to the condo soon."

Amy checked her phone. "Wow, you're not kidding. We're barely going to make it back by the time they get there."

"I've had so much fun chatting with you, I completely forgot we had a schedule to keep. Looks like I'll be too late to catch my yoga class too."

"Are you sure? You still have time," Amy nervously insisted.

"Yes, I'm sure. I'd rather be sure you've got things ready for the move anyway. Be there in case you need help with the movers."

As they left, Amy gave her mother a worried glance, but Taryn gave it no mind, assuming it just had to do with the movers. Its meaning finally registered though, when they pulled up in front of the condo and she saw that Wyatt's car was parked there.

"I'm so sorry, Mom. Dad offered to help and we both thought you'd be gone to your class by now."

Taryn gritted her teeth, annoyed that she would have to deal with her ex, furious that Amy had arranged for him to be in the condo without even asking permission. But in the interest of harmony, she forced herself to give her daughter a smile. "It's okay, honey. We'll just make the best of it."

Make the best of it, she thought as they walked to meet Wyatt. *That's what I've always done. Hold myself in, avoid ruffling other people's feathers, go along with whatever my husband or my kids want. And here I am again ...*

Wyatt hugged Amy, then sheepishly said, "Hello, Taryn. I didn't think you'd be home. I'm awfully sorry to intrude here ..." His eyes dropped to the pavement.

Her face tensed and her eyes were steely, but as they entered the building and moved toward the elevator, Taryn managed to say, "If it's what Amy wants, then that's what she'll get."

Walking into her apartment, though, Taryn suddenly felt violated at the presence of him in *her* space. This place, where she had spent so many months crying, trying to understand, crawling back to her own sense of self, was now tainted by the very person who had caused her so much pain. She wanted to scream.

Instead, she turned to Wyatt and said, "You can stay here in the kitchen while Amy and I make sure she's got everything done in her room." Taryn desperately wanted him to be in her home as little as possible. She wished she'd had the nerve to tell him to wait outside.

There was a knock on the door then; the movers had arrived. Taryn let two tall muscular young men inside and pointed to Amy. "She's in charge of this operation." Taryn had tried to make that sound light, but failed miserably. To her own ears it came out full of resentment, but no one else seemed to have taken it that way.

Wyatt immediately jumped in. "No, Taryn, I came here to help Amy, so I'll just go with them, help her with the last miscellaneous things." He turned to his daughter. "Lead the way, honey." As he had for so many years, Wyatt automatically took control of the situation, dismissing Taryn's wishes.

Amy hesitated, waiting for Taryn to affirm what she'd said before and contradict Wyatt's command. When Taryn said nothing, she echoed her father, and motioned the men to her room, "in here."

While the others busied themselves with the packing and moving boxes to the van waiting downstairs, Taryn sat in the kitchen staring at the wall, unbidden memories flooding her mind.

She saw herself talking to a friend on the arts council, heard the friend telling her, "You're so lucky. You have the perfect marriage, such a perfect husband." Taryn had believed it too at the time, felt herself living the fairy tale of happily ever after. An image of their wedding flashed through her mind: Wyatt's eyes so full of love, her own heart full as well while they spoke their vows to each other.

She saw Wyatt's face again fifteen years later at their anniversary dinner. This time his eyes would barely meet hers and instead of the intimate loving conversation of their early years, they talked only about details of the kitchen renovation they were planning.

She saw that horrible night when Wyatt came home late— he'd been working a lot of late nights recently, she'd realized—to announce that he'd been seeing their friend Greta and wanted a divorce. It was a 9.0 earthquake that shook her to the core. She'd collapsed on the floor like a blow-up doll whose plug had been pulled, letting all the air escape. Air. Yes, that's what she'd been filled with for years, just a lot of air. No real substance, nothing solid, just an empty space giving temporary form to a shell. There wasn't even water to make tears.

He'd ripped her to shreds, ripped their life to shreds, in the most hurtful way possible.

Now she sat watching her dear daughter's leaving, watching Wyatt run the show, as he usually did. Feelings of anger at Wyatt, frustration with herself for letting him override her, sorrow for the loss of her daughter swirled madly inside her, and she felt herself shrinking into despair. Not since the night of Wyatt's announcement about his affair had she felt so small.

Finally Amy could no longer ignore the looks of anguish on her mother's face. Guiltily, she turned to Wyatt and said, "Dad, I think you should go on to the new apartment and I'll meet you there as soon as I'm sure the movers have the truck loaded."

The uncertain look on Wyatt's face said that wasn't how he and Amy had planned it, before they knew Taryn would be home. His glance at Amy told Taryn he'd expected to leave the condo along with their daughter. But the finality in his daughter's voice warned him not to push it.

"Fine, Amy. I'll see you soon." He turned on his heel and headed to the door. "Bye, Taryn. Again, sorry."

"Bye," was all Taryn could manage to say.

Wyatt left. Amy smiled wanly at her mother and went back to her room to instruct the movers. After a few minutes, she left too. She could barely look Taryn in the eye, but she mouthed the word "sorry" as she closed the door.

Taryn stood, frozen, for what seemed to her like an eternity. Caught in non-time, non-space, the old feelings of impotent emptiness at having relinquished her own power to Wyatt washed over her. How could she have done that to herself yet again? After so much time had passed since the split? Had nothing changed for her at all? Was this nightmare ever going to end?

She walked slowly to her bedroom and fell back on her bed, tears of misery trailing down her cheeks.

September finally arrived and Taryn began packing for the "adventure" Paige had roped her into. All in all the art show had gone pretty well. So many paintings and sculptures were sold that the council had made most of the money they'd need for the coming year. It was a resounding success, and the volunteers celebrated well into the night at a nearby restaurant. Only the entrance of Greta, for a brief moment across the room, had marred the experience. The flood of painful emotions instantly brought tears to Taryn's eyes, and she'd fled to the restroom until she could recover, fervently wishing she could find a way out of the anguish.

Thinking of that moment, as she folded sweaters and jeans, morphed into the uneasy feelings she'd had about what might be coming on this trip. As there had been nothing she could do about it during the art show, Taryn had generally tried to push the troublesome thoughts away, but now they returned in full force. She was inexplicably both excited and frightened by what might happen. She tried to talk herself out of the uneasiness. *I mean, how deep or life-changing could a dude ranch be?* Especially as she had no intention of falling off a horse, as Amy had warned her not to do.

As she went to the dresser one last time for underwear and her nightgown, her gaze fell momentarily on her own reflection in the mirror. Her lips were thinner than they used to be, and she had little crow's feet just beginning to show. It was her eyes that had changed the most over time. In them she saw the joys, and struggles, and monotony, and sorrow, and pain, and love, and gratefulness of her life thus far lived. For the last three years, all clouded over by melancholy and doubt. The feeling that her past was truly *past* now welled up strongly, and with no sense of what her future might be, she felt caught in a disquieting limbo. She gave herself a shaky smile and went back to her task.

A glass of Merlot and an enthusiastic text from Paige helped steady her nerves, and she resolved to face whatever was coming her way.

Chapter

2

Paige *had already been picked up* by the Lyft driver when the car arrived at Taryn's condo, and she squealed excitedly when Taryn got in the back seat with her.

"Oh, we are going to have so much fun!"

"Okay," Taryn laughed. "Settle down, girl. You're going to hit your head on the roof of this car if you keep bouncing like that."

"I don't care. I am so looking forward to this."

Taryn smiled. "Me too actually. After all the busyness of the last month, I'm ready for some serious R and R."

"I talked to the ranch, and they're going to give us a few hours in town when we land to go shopping for some genuine cowgirl duds. We don't want to look like a couple of city slickers!"

"Yeah like us walking in with brand new boots on isn't going to tip them off," Taryn chuckled at her friend. However, she had to admit it could really be fun—trying on a new persona. She'd been stuck half in and half out of the person she'd been as a "married woman" for far too long, and "divorced woman" still didn't fit quite right, however true. It was definitely time for a change. *Why not try cowgirl on?*

⌒

The plane ride went about as smoothly as air travel could go considering modern day security and crowded airport hassles.

Taryn loved flying, especially the takeoff. She'd let Paige know to keep quiet until they were in the air. When the seatbelt sign went off though, Taryn was still staring out the window, for far longer than she usually did.

Paige nudged her gently. "Okay, girl, what gives? You're usually all chatty by now."

Taryn turned and shrugged her shoulders resignedly. "God, Paige. I didn't want to tell you this. I'm so embarrassed. Remember when I said I took Amy to lunch before she moved out?"

"Yeah," said Paige, wondering how that could have her friend so upset.

"Well I left out the part about Wyatt showing up to help her move." She dropped her eyes.

Paige let out a slow "whew."

"He wasn't there for long, but it was so jarring—having him in my space. I'm still a bit mad at Amy for inviting him like that."

"No kidding. Did you have some words with her about it?"

"No. I know she got it, because she wouldn't even look at me when she left. But that wasn't the worst, really." She cringed. "Paige, Wyatt took control like he always does—waltzing into my home uninvited by me, ignoring me when I told him to stay in the kitchen, going right into Amy's room to help her pack—and I just let him. *I* wanted to be the one who helped Amy with her things. I didn't even try to stand my ground, in my own condo. I ..." Taryn's eyes filled with tears and she looked away quickly, out the window, so others couldn't see.

Paige reached out and put her hand on Taryn's arm. "Oh, Taryn. I'm so sorry."

She didn't know what else to say. For so many years she had watched Taryn back down whenever Wyatt asserted himself, and no matter how often she tried to shore Taryn up, encourage her to use her voice, it had made no difference. She knew that until Taryn decided—on her own—to take charge of her life, it never would.

Taryn turned to Paige beseechingly. "Have I really not grown at all since the ... Have I learned nothing in all this time?"

"I'm glad you told me. And yes, you have learned a lot. This is just showing you you're not done yet." Then, as a mother knows to distract an upset child, "I think we shouldn't worry about that for a while. We're on our way to having some serious fun. Let's focus on horses and cowboys and spa days."

Taryn nodded and smiled as her mood brightened. "Agreed."

In spite of how close they'd been for so many years, Paige had always been somewhat of an enigma to Taryn. Her grandfather had emigrated from India, so she'd inherited long straight black hair and dark brown eyes, along with a petite figure and light brown skin Taryn had always envied. In college Paige had been a wild card, and in many ways she still was. Her family was quite wealthy, so she hadn't really needed to work for a living. After graduation she'd tried making a career in journalism, but it didn't take. Too confining. She'd since devoted herself to volunteer work. And her son.

Her marriage had been brief, to say the least. Derek was only six months old when Jack was killed by a drunk driver. Taryn had watched with fascination as her friend grieved for maybe a minute, then went on with her life with her son. Derek was obviously the true love of her life. And in spite of her free spirit inclinations, she was an excellent mother, always seeming to find that delicate balance between helping and hovering.

Because Paige was determined never to marry again, her dating life was a constant source of entertainment for Taryn. Men of all ages, occupations and physical types came and went; Paige was clearly set on experiencing a very wide variety. Few even made it past the second date (or second base), and none lasted much longer than that. Taryn met only a small percentage, and Derek even less. "All in good fun," Paige would often exclaim. She was such a contrast to the solidly married Taryn that they frequently marveled at how they'd managed to stay friends all these years. Finally, in jest, they'd decided it was their shared love of Merlot.

Taryn cherished the relationship she had with Paige. To have someone who knew her so thoroughly was a gift beyond measure.

The rest of the flight was spent talking about Paige's son Derek, who had recently landed his idea of the perfect job. And he'd met a girl Paige thought had real possibilities.

"Charlotte is a real gem. She holds her own with Derek, doesn't take any sass from him. But she's also so sweet. You'll see when you meet her. They're so cute together, holding hands, kissing each other on the cheek." Paige sighed. "Young love, in all its glory."

"I'm really happy for him. Now that he's got that job, he's probably ready to settle down. Do you think they're that serious yet?"

Paige considered the question. "Yeah, I think they might be." She grew pensive as she added, "Guess he's not gonna be my little boy for much longer."

Taryn patted her on the arm. "No, he's not."

Paige sighed, then cocked her head, and her face turned to the impish look Taryn knew all too well. "Maybe Derek's not the only one who could find a new love. Never know who you might meet at the dude ranch ..."

In exasperation Taryn retorted, "Cut it out, Paige. I am so not ready for that, and you know it." She turned the tables on her friend. "Maybe it's you who will finally find love there."

Paige opened her mouth, ready to protest, but no sound escaped as her eyes went wide with acceptance of the possibility.

A van from J's River Ranch met them at the Steamboat Springs airport. The handsome cowboy who emerged from the driver's seat introduced himself as Dustin, the ranch manager. He was lanky and lean with shoulder-length light brown hair pulled back in a tail and a barely-there beard. His eyes sparkled with a joy that can only come from loving the life lived. Paige was instantly hooked. She gushed all over him as he put their bags in the back, and Taryn would have been a bit embarrassed for her friend, but Dustin was obviously enjoying it. *Coming attractions of another Paige show* thought Taryn. She smiled.

The little country and western wear store Dustin took them to didn't look like much from the outside, but inside was a treasure trove of just what they were hoping for. It didn't take long for Paige to decide to buy a whole new wardrobe for herself and Taryn too. Dustin had come in with them and with some trepidation he let himself be talked into judging the fashion try-on sessions. First came the dresses.

"Okay, Dustin," Paige said. "I've picked out five. You have to choose the best three."

"Oh, lordy, woman," protested Dustin. "This sounds like a trap. What if I pick the wrong three?"

"Just pick the ones you like the most. I'm aiming to please *you*." Paige batted her eyes at him and he turned crimson, coughed. Taryn doubled over with laughter.

"Better get used to this, Dustin. She's got her sights on you."

Surprisingly, Dustin had pretty good taste. He picked the three Taryn would have picked for Paige—a pure white, loose fitting, cold-shoulder dress with delicate lace across the chest and arms, a fitted faux suede dress with full length long-fringed sleeves in a deep wine color, and a denim shirt dress with decorative stitching and a leather belt. Meanwhile Taryn had found a couple of fun dresses for herself, which Dustin approved of as well.

Then it was on to jeans and shirts. Paige of course went for the embellished jeans, with silver studs in lacy designs on the back pockets. Her tops were lacy, embroidered or ruffled, in bright festive colors. Taryn chose the more modest and practical classic jeans, but she found several shirts with a little more flare, with fringe and embroidered designs. And a blue plaid shirt with western style piping.

Boots and hats completed their outfits. To contrast with her blond hair, Taryn chose black for both feet and head. Her slouch boots featured harness studs and star concho accents, and her hat had a band with black leatherette lacing and star conchos to echo the boots. Paige chose an inlay boot in soft turquoise covered by a light brown floral design and delicate topstitching. She managed to find a hat in the same colors and style, with a turquoise inlay on the crown, and a hatband sporting metal buckles on either side of a turquoise stone accent.

No way was anyone going to take either of these friends as serious Colorado cowgirls, but they were definitely having a blast with the western styles. Taryn found herself relaxing happily into this crazy trip. Paige was about to start looking through the jackets when Dustin spoke up.

"Okay, ladies, we gotta wrap this up. One of the other guests is arriving at the airport shortly and we're picking him up before we head to the ranch. You have ten minutes to figure out which things you're actually going to buy and get them paid for."

"Ah Dustin, but we're having such fun," pouted Paige.

"Darlin', don't give me that face now. Be a good girl," teased Dustin.

Taryn grimaced. *Jeez, already he's got her eating out of his hand. This guy might be just what Paige needs, keep her in line a little. Not that she won't wind him round her finger later...*

Paige flashed Dustin a wicked smile, but she did as he asked. After making a rather large dent in her credit card, they piled the bags in the van and headed back to the airport. Paige sat in the front seat, her full attention on Dustin. Finally he turned to her and with a stern voice said, "Look Paige. I know me and you are havin' a good time flirting and all. But ranch hands aren't allowed to 'fraternize' with the guests. You'll get me in big trouble if you keep this up in front of everyone."

Paige grimaced. "Are you saying you want me to back off you altogether?"

Dustin chuckled. "I think you know the answer to that. No. But I gotta be careful."

"Ooh." She brightened. "So we have to be sneaky. I can do that." She put her hand on his arm while Dustin, and Taryn in the back, laughed heartily.

Just as they pulled up outside the terminal, Taryn caught sight of a man walking quickly through the door. As soon as he saw the van his face broke out in a wide grin. From the back seat Taryn gave him a quick study. Short brown hair, thin mouth and a confident, purposeful walk suggested he was all business, in spite of the casual jeans and plaid shirt he had on. As he reached the van, she thought he looked about forty. His intelligent green eyes, fringed with long straight eyelashes, were his most striking feature. For half a second, she almost thought it was Wyatt—his energy was so similar. Taryn found herself responding to his winning smile, as she had to Wyatt in their early days. Then she came to her senses. Taryn had had her fill of that personable, take-charge type. Her intuition told her she needed to steer clear of this guy.

"That one's for you, girl," whispered Paige.

"As if," Taryn huffed. "I am so not looking to get involved with anyone."

"Yeah," Paige taunted her.

He strode to the van and peeked in the window while Dustin took care of his bags.

"Hello, ladies. Are you as ready to have a good time as I am?"

His eyes were locked on Taryn as he said this and she flushed, turned to Paige.

"We sure are. I'm Paige, and this is Taryn. What's your name?"

"Eric, ma'am. Pleased to meet you." He made a motion like tipping his hat to them. Then he slid onto the seat beside Taryn.

Dustin got in, too, and turned to his passengers.

"I'll be taking you to the ranch now, then I have to come back and pick up a couple more guests. Which means one of our wranglers will be showing you to your cabins. It's about a forty-minute drive so settle in and enjoy the ride."

Paige pursed her lips and frowned, clearly not wanting to be separated from Dustin while he made the next airport run.

"Why don't we all just hang out at a bar nearby till the others get here? It would save you a trip," she said hopefully.

Seeing the expression on her friend's face, Taryn quickly agreed. "That sounds great to me. What about you, Eric?"

"Sure. Give me a chance to get to know you gals," he said, looking straight at Taryn.

Dustin was clearly relieved to get out of all that driving. "Thank you. I'll let my boss, Jesse, know, and I'm sure he'd be happy to buy the first round."

Taryn felt a sudden and unexpected tingle at the mention of Jesse's name.

"Good, that's settled then," said Paige, quite pleased with herself. "Any place around here that's an old-fashioned cowboy bar?"

"No, ma'am, we don't have any of those in these parts," drawled Dustin with a grin. "Only about a dozen I can think of in a five-mile radius. I know just where to take you."

He called the ranch, told Jesse the change in plans. Sure enough, his boss was quite happy to have the ranch foot the bill for a few drinks.

They did the usual chitchat on the short ride to the bar—where are you from, have you been to Colorado before. Eric, having lived his whole life on the east coast, was clearly excited to experience the West and his enthusiasm was contagious. Everyone was in good spirits when they arrived.

Taryn loved Smithy's Saloon as soon as she walked in, and she knew it was just what Paige had wanted. This authentic nineteenth century bar would be pure inspiration for Hollywood, she thought. The battered brick building was full of very well-used solid wood chairs around tables with the carved names of patrons from decades of drunken nights. The owners had bucked the modern day habit of plastering neon beer signs all over the walls and instead had pictures of old-time Colorado towns in heavy frames. The bar itself was made of rough-hewn lumber; no fancy stuff here. In the corner, with a small dance floor in front of it, she saw an old jukebox. It still worked and was currently playing a Luke Bryant ballad. Taryn smiled at Paige, who grinned and squeezed Dustin's arm delightedly.

They chose a table against the wall with a good view of the room. Dustin, being the gentleman cowboy, pulled out a chair for Paige. Eric was obviously unused to this ritual, but clumsily did the same for Taryn. As she sat, he put his hand on her shoulder in a familiar manner. Taryn bristled.

A waitress in worn jeans and a Smithy's Saloon T-shirt approached.

"Hi y'all. My name's Susan. What can I get you folks to drink?"

Paige spoke first, gestured to Taryn. "We'll have two glasses of Merlot please."

"And I'll have a coke. I'm driving," said Dustin.

Eric grinned. "What is it cowboys drink? Whiskey? I'll have a double."

"Okey doke. Be right back," Susan said as she spun round on one heel and headed for the bar. In just a few minutes she returned with a full tray and served their drinks.

"Cheers," Paige exclaimed, raising her glass.

Everyone joined the toast then took a sip of their drinks. Except Eric, who poured half his whiskey in his mouth all at once. Suddenly he sputtered, then started coughing uncontrollably. Susan had watched this greenhorn take the large gulp and was already on her way over with a glass of water.

"Holy shit, that's some strong stuff," Eric struggled to say.

Taryn and Paige couldn't help but laugh. Dustin, having seen this sort of behavior many times from other ranch guests, managed to keep a straight face. But he gave Paige a wink.

"Well this sure is a lot more fun than driving back and forth to the ranch all afternoon. Thanks for suggesting we hang out here." Then turning to Eric he added, "You doing all right now? That was quite the slug you took."

"Yeah, I'm fine. Just caught me by surprise is all. I think I can handle a shot of whiskey, thank you very much," Eric said defensively.

Smoothly ignoring the tone of that remark, Dustin asked Eric what he did for living.

Eric brightened instantly. "I'm the founder and CEO of Sparkle." Three blank faces stared back at him.

"Sparkle. The app everyone's talking about. Where you can let the world know all of your accomplishments. A perpetual resume, if you will. Surely you've heard of Sparkle. Everyone worthwhile is on it." He seemed genuinely amazed none of them knew about his great invention.

Finally Taryn spoke. "No, sorry. I've been kind of out of the loop for a while."

"Well. You're definitely missing out. I could set you up, maybe even give you a personal recommendation." He gave her a cocky smile.

His eager, over-confident air flooded her with memories of Wyatt. Still so young when they'd met, she'd been uncertain of herself and where her life was to go. The arrival of Wyatt's enthusiasm for life and his carefully planned goals seemed to fill all the empty spaces in her, instantaneously, and she'd settled into place with nary a thought about what she might *really* have wanted to be in this life. Following him made her feel secure, and important. So she let him make the decisions, over and over, until she barely knew how to make any of her own any more. Once, just after the divorce, a friend on the arts council had asked her if she preferred shrimp or scallops for the event appetizer. Taryn automatically blurted out "shrimp," then suddenly realized that was always Wyatt's choice; she really didn't have any idea what she herself liked best. That shock had started the slow process of finding her own self again, of making all the tiny choices she'd abdicated for so long. She looked Eric fully in the face and knew she could never go there again.

"Thanks, but I don't really have any use for something like ... Sparkle? ... right now."

"Oh, well you will in the future. Why not get started now?" Eric was insistent.

She had to do something to stem this onslaught. She turned to Dustin and pleaded. "Tell us something about the ranch, you know, its history and such."

Paige caught her drift and asked, "How long have you worked there?"

"About five years now."

"Where were you before? And where did you come from?" Paige wanted to know all about this hot cowboy.

"Whoa, slow down. I grew up in Texas, on the plains in the panhandle. Summers I worked on a cattle ranch and got hooked on the whole cowboy thing. Even did some rodeo for a while."

Taryn jumped in. "What events?"

"Mostly bronc riding, but some roping too. I had to quit when I broke a leg and it didn't heal a hundred percent."

"What got you to Colorado then?" Paige asked.

"Friend of mine set me up with a job running cattle. That only lasted a couple years though. I didn't like the way the owner ran his business and how he treated the animals. So I left. One of the ranch hands heard about this dude ranch that was looking for a manager, and here I am."

"Well I'm glad." Paige gushed, then blushed.

Dustin grinned. "Me too actually. Jesse is the best boss I've ever had. He's honest, hard-working and it's obvious he has a lot of respect for the people who work for him. He's a good friend now."

Taryn again felt a deep stir at hearing Jesse's name. Quickly she shifted the topic. "Tell us more about the ranch. What will we be doing this week?"

Before Dustin could answer, his phone rang. "Yeah? ... Huh ... Okay."

He turned to the others. "Jesse says the people we were going to pick up missed their plane and decided to cancel their week at the ranch. Sounded like there might be something else going on, but at any rate we can just go straight on from here. So whenever y'all are ready."

As the van pulled off the highway, Taryn felt a shiver of anticipation run through her. The ranch's long gravel drive was lined with majestic Colorado blue spruce trees, and ended in a wide circle around the most amazing fountain she had ever seen. Twenty feet high on a huge array of boulders stood a sculpture of a bull elk, head raised to the sky. Water poured from the points of his mighty antlers and tumbled over the rocks to the river-rock filled pool below. The serene power and beauty of the elk thrilled her in a way she could not readily understand.

When finally she could tear her gaze away from the fountain, she took in the ranch itself. Most of the buildings were log cabin style. The main lodge was one story, with a wrap-around porch for easy lounging. Taryn could see three porch swings just from where she was in the van. The wide plank steps were flanked by evergreen shrubs and colorful flowers hardy enough to withstand the Colorado winters. It felt to her like a warm, welcoming farmhouse.

Off to one side was the barn, almost as large as the lodge. Surrounded by weathered fences with wagon wheels near the gates, it was painted the dark red so popular in the west. Farther out from the barn was a pasture where several horses munched on the green grass, their tails flicking away the inevitable flies. A river ran through the south side of the pasture; Taryn could see the horseback riding trail on the other side. And up in the hills behind the lodge, Taryn saw the many guest cabins, nestled in among dark green pine trees, and aspens just turning their golds and coppers of fall. Taking in the peaceful energy of the ranch, she took a deep breath and relaxed as the van came to a stop in front of the lodge.

Chapter

3

He was *the first thing Taryn* saw when she walked in the door of the main lodge. His body was lean and fit from hours spent tending horses and keeping the ranch in top shape. Dressed in worn boots, black jeans, and a red plaid shirt, Jesse was every bit the picture of a Colorado rancher. He wore a black cowboy hat, which made his deep brown eyes look like pools of melted chocolate. As his head turned to gaze directly at her, her body quivered at the connection.

He cleared his throat and removed his hat, revealing his thick brown hair, and welcomed his new guests in a deep melodic voice that quickly made them all feel at ease. As he spoke of meal times and activities and ground rules, it was evident that he genuinely respected these strangers who had come to spend their time at his ranch. He was warm, and funny, smiling often with a twinkle in his eye. When he told them they'd be driving cattle to Wyoming at the end of the week, they all laughed nervously until they realized he was teasing.

Yet Taryn sensed a certain reserve in his manner, a protective wall around him. And she wondered at the contrast between his outward warmth and inward vulnerability.

"So now that I've told you a bit about what we'll be doing this week, help yourselves to the wine and cheese bar, maybe get to know your fellow ranch-mates. When you're ready, Dustin, Jim and Larry here will show you to your cabins. Remember dinner is at six o'clock."

Taryn watched him furtively while Paige prattled on about Dustin, who was talking quietly to Jesse. The two men glanced at Paige from time to time and it was obvious the conversation was about her. A smile lit up Jesse's face as he gently slapped Dustin on the back. He was clearly pleased for his friend, and Taryn caught a glimpse of how much Jesse cared for the people who worked for him, as Dustin had said. Jesse's laughter was heartfelt and sexy, to Taryn's ears at least. Dustin reacted differently, play-punching his boss on the arm as he moved away.

Seeing Dustin free again, Paige left Taryn and re-attached herself to her handsome cowboy. Taryn smiled and shook her head. *Girl's in full-on claim-her-man mode. This is going to be one interesting week.* She started toward the wine bar that had been set up along one wall of the lodge.

One of the staff was just walking through the swinging door to the kitchen carrying a tray of wine glasses and an open bottle of wine. She'd nearly made it out, but the door caught her left heel and she lost her balance. She did a good job keeping the glasses on the tray, but the bottle toppled over, spilling red wine on a braided rug. Taryn rushed to pick up the bottle, trying to keep as much of the wine as possible from pouring out. When she had it upright, she grabbed some napkins from the table, dropped to the floor and started dabbing at the rug.

"Do you have any club soda?" she asked the poor woman still holding the tray. "It should help get most of this up."

Hastily the tray was set down and the woman disappeared into the kitchen again. Taryn continued to soak up the wine with the napkins she could find.

Jesse had watched it all with fascination. He'd never had a guest react so quickly to assist his staff. Most guests expected to be served, not do anything remotely resembling work. Yet this one, sensitive to the server's plight, had immediately helped, taken charge, was on her knees cleaning. It was a glimpse into her naturally caring, humble character, and he was deeply appreciative.

When the job was done, Taryn looked up to see Jesse staring intently at her, the admiration in his expression not to be missed. She blushed, quickly turning her head in hopes he hadn't seen.

Jesse started. *Was that a reaction I just saw? I thought it was just me, drawn to her. God what is it about her? She's blond, and I don't do blondes any more, not since Veronica. But her eyes ... such a deep soulful blue. I could so get lost in those ... Dude, get off it. Really. You can't be going there, especially with a guest.*

Larry came up then to work out the details of the trail ride for the next morning and Jesse was grateful for the distraction. Still, when Taryn passed by on her way to join Paige and Dustin, he felt her strongly. A warmth rushed through him and an image of the energetic bonds between them flashed through his mind.

Taryn felt it too. Something about this quiet, private, confident man fascinated her. And though she tried to convince herself it was just because it would be fun to get to the bottom of why he'd built that wall, the tingling from their first eye contact had escalated, spreading like a brush fire in her veins. She was grateful she'd just passed him by before the hot flush reached her face.

❧

Paige quickly decided she didn't really care about wine and cheese, and grabbed Dustin's arm to make sure he would be the one to show her to her cabin. She begged Taryn to come along. "We can meet the others at dinner later."

As soon as they were out of earshot of the lodge, Dustin stopped and turned to Paige.

"Darlin' I really do like it when you get sassy and sexy with me. But remember what I said on the way to the airport earlier? I can't be seen getting all clingy with the guests. I know I can't control what you do—oh lordy, I do know that," he winked. "But I can't be responding to your advances, well not when others are around. You got that?"

Paige pouted and batted her eyes at him. But she nodded.

They wound their way up the hillside behind the main lodge. Dustin headed for two side-by-side cabins surrounded by trees, making for a serene and secluded feeling. Taryn loved it. As they entered her cabin, she saw that her luggage had already been brought up. Though small, the cabin's interior was cozy and inviting. The bed was covered in what looked to be a handmade quilt in soft shades of blues and greens and browns—a log cabin design if she remembered her quilting patterns right. A bathroom in the corner, while decorated in a rustic style, seemed almost brand new. The room was heated by a small gas stove near the door with a comfy chair nearby, perfect for snuggling up with a good book. It was simple, clean and welcoming, and Taryn felt instantly at home.

As she settled in and began unpacking her things, she could hear Dustin and Paige happily talking next door in Paige's room. She smiled when she heard Paige giggle, then it got very quiet. *That didn't take long. Well done, Paige. I hope you know what you're in for, Dustin.*

Then she grimaced. When it got noisy over there later she was liable to hear every bit of it. *Ah well, at least one of us will have some action.*

Taryn gave it about two minutes after she heard the door slam to be sure Dustin had left, then she walked over to Paige's room and sat down in a chair that looked very much like the one in her cabin.

"So ... looks like your week is going to be interesting." She raised an eyebrow and grinned.

"Yours could be too. Eric has obviously taken a shine to you, even though you've been a bit standoffish with him." Hands on hips, she half scolded her friend.

"Jeez, Paige, I just can't go there. I just can't. He reminds me too much of Wyatt. All arrogant and pushy. I've had enough of that," Taryn said tersely.

"Wow. I never thought of Wyatt as arrogant," Paige mused.

"That may be a bit strong. Over-confident is better. Like so sure of himself that you feel you have to go along with whatever he wants. Like your opinion would be utterly irrelevant, so why bother expressing it. I need to be around that kind of energy again like I need a hole in the head."

Paige reflected. "Okay, I see that. What are you going to do about Sparkle boy then?"

Taryn chuckled. "What a great nickname. I'll never be able to think of him as Eric now." She put her head on her hand and sighed. "I honestly don't know. If he's true to form, he won't readily take no for an answer. Wyatt sure didn't." Her eyes pleaded with her friend. "I'm going to need some help here."

"I'll do my best. Hey what did you think of the owner, Jesse? Kind of a dish, huh?"

Taryn hesitated for a second. She didn't dare tell her friend about the connection she'd felt to the intriguing man who was their host.

Better to keep it casual and avoid the certain goading Paige would lay on her if she detected interest. "Well, he's handsome, no doubt about that. Doesn't give off any vibes that he'd want to get involved with anyone though. Bit of a wall there."

Ever one to rise to a challenge, Paige pushed. "I don't know. Walls crumble. I think you two could be good together. Did you see that look he gave you? Ooh, whee."

Exasperation edged Taryn's voice. "Cut it out, Paige. What would he want with me? I'm still a mess from ... before. And I'll say it again—I am *not* looking for anyone."

"But Jesse isn't 'anyone.' I can see it, even if you can't. Jesse is seriously hot, and definitely into you." Paige pleaded with her friend to open up a little.

Taryn rolled her eyes. "Aargh ... please give it a rest. I really don't want another man in my life right now." She jumped to her feet and grabbed Paige by the wrist. "Let's go meet the others before dinner."

Paige shrugged and walked through the door. Taryn followed, torn between excitement and dread at Paige's remarks.

❧

Walking back to the lodge with Paige, Taryn fully took in the energy of the ranch again. Solar powered miniature lanterns lined the meandering stone paths that connected the cabins to the lodge. She imagined what they must look like at night, friendly guiding lights that might show her the way. A feeling of warmth flowed through her, and she smiled in contentment at being here.

Halfway there they met up with Dustin again. Paige started to latch onto his arm, but caught herself and moved away to a "respectable" distance. He gave her a grateful smile.

A small building Taryn hadn't seen before caught her eye. Tucked away among the rocks and trees, it was larger than the guest cabins and clearly set apart from them.

"Hey, Dustin, what's that?" Taryn asked.

"Oh, that's Jesse's house."

Her curiosity kicked into high gear. "It looks really nice. What's it like inside?"

"No one knows. Jesse never invites people up there. Wants it to be his own private place, I guess."

"Hummm," was all Taryn could think to respond, remembering her sense that he kept a shield around himself.

As she walked in the door of the lodge, Taryn realized she had hardly noticed the interior when she first arrived, so engrossed had she been with being in Jesse's presence. Now she looked around curiously. Immediately she was hit with a sense of the pioneer days. In the sitting areas, braided rugs covered the wide plank wood floors. Comfy leather chairs had flowered plushy pillows. At one end of the room was a large brick fireplace flanked by old-time crockery—a butter churn and pitchers of various sizes and colors. On the polished wood mantel were statues of horses and carved wooden cowboy hats. Above it was a collection of rodeo buckles in rustic frames. Walls were wood paneled from the floor to a chair rail, and painted a pale sage green above. Numerous pictures hung on them, all depicting the rugged lifestyle of the people who had settled in this area. Dining tables were oval, seating eight to ten each, for a "family" experience for the guests. The soft lighting from antler chandeliers and sconces made the large room feel intimate and inviting. Taryn was reminded of Jesse's sensual voice as he welcomed his guests, and a rush of excitement ran through her.

Paige tugged her arm and they made their way to the table set for their first night's dinner, sitting down across from three Asian guests.

Eric moved quickly toward the place beside Taryn. To her immense relief, he lost out to a casually but impeccably dressed brunette woman with an air of easy warmth who introduced herself as Kathy. Taryn liked her instantly.

"Hi, I'm Taryn. And this is Paige, the friend who dragged me here." She grinned affectionately as she said it.

"So what's the real story of how you got here?" Kathy was curious.

Paige jumped in with details about the charity auction and Taryn's initial reluctance to come. Kathy's ears perked up at the mention of the arts council.

"That's so cool you're involved in the art world. Me too. I've been an artist, well, for as long as I can remember. Had a few shows in Kansas City. Mostly landscapes."

"Wow," Paige said. "I'd love to see some of your work some time. I know lots of gallery owners in the Seattle area. If you're interested in showing there, I could maybe give you an introduction."

Kathy smiled in grateful surprise. "That would be amazing. Thank you. Maybe after dinner I could grab my laptop and show you my latest creations. We could talk more then." Addressing Taryn, she asked, "Are you on the arts council too?"

"No, not anymore," Taryn said with a touch of melancholy in her voice. "I help out with the annual art show, but kind of left the rest to Paige."

"So what do you do now?"

"I guess you'd have to say that I'm an ex corporate wife, somewhat adrift right now." Anxious to stop further talk about herself, Taryn pointed to the tall, ruggedly handsome man sitting across from Kathy. "That's your husband, right? How did you two wind up here?"

"Ah, yes. Mark and I have been married for coming up fifteen years now. Every year we leave the kids with my parents and spend a couple weeks, just us. Gives us time to really re-connect. This year we decided to drive through Nebraska and Wyoming, then try out the dude ranch experience here in Colorado. Not much chance to do that near K.C."

Kathy turned then to include the Asian woman, who introduced herself as Ichika, in the conversation. Taryn felt Kathy's words hit her hard in the gut—"just us." She and Wyatt had never taken that kind of time to be together as a couple. Everything was always about work and the kids. No wonder they'd not been able to keep going. Without any re-charging, the relationship had run out of juice. She pushed the thoughts away to stop the urge to cry, and focused on what Ichika was saying.

"... wanted to see the 'wild west' so we asked for an extra week after the conference as vacation. I am really excited to ride a horse. In Japan horseback riding is not easy to find, and very expensive."

"What conference did you go to?" Kathy asked.

One of the men next to Ichika broke in. "The conference was about all aspects of how countries are dealing with their trash, and had speakers from many professions. The company we work for in Tokyo is developing a satellite that will clean up the debris everyone's space programs have left up there. It is an interesting and relatively new field with lots of challenges, as you can imagine. And I am Kaito." He bowed his head slightly.

"I am Tadao," said the man next to him. "Kaito and Ichika have worked for the company for many years. I have only been there for one year. But it is exciting to be creating—how do you say it?—cutting edge technology."

Taryn was intrigued. "That sounds amazing. I for one would like to thank you, and your company, for taking on that task. I've often wondered what was happening with all the junk left up there."

Ichika was about to say something when Jesse walked in with a slightly built man who looked like he belonged in a reggae band. The long dreads, deep brown skin and twinkling eyes made Taryn like him instantly. They were such a contrast to the usual Colorado look that she marveled at the richness of the diversity in this gathering. *Wonder who that is, and how he got here!*

Jesse explained in his introduction that the now widely smiling man was Bobby, the ranch chef. As Taryn made eye contact, Bobby cocked his head, holding her for a moment in a heartfelt gaze. Then he gave her a friendly wink. The simple gesture warmed her heart and she winked back at him.

Then he addressed the guests. "We want to make sure your dining experience at the ranch is top notch, so if any of you have dietary concerns or requests—vegetarian, lactose intolerance, gluten free—just let me know and we'll try our best to get you what you need." He smiled again. "One Love."

Jesse put his hand on Bobby's shoulder briefly as he finished, and Taryn could feel the genuine admiration that connected them.

With that, Bobby waved to everyone and quickly left to resume his duties in the kitchen. Jesse left too, but not before casting an extended glance at Taryn.

Taryn had just caught the end of Jesse's look, but had no time to process her reaction as plates of food were entering the room on the arms of staff. Bobby had evidently gone all out for this dinner and the smells were tantalizing. Suddenly all the chatter stopped and there was a contented silence as everyone dug into the Jamaican jerk chicken, slaw, and herbed potatoes. After a few minutes Bobby peeked out to see how things were going and Taryn gave him a thumbs up. He grinned back at her gratefully.

Mark broke the silence.

"So. Eric was it? What do you do?"

Eric brightened immediately and launched into his favorite topic—Sparkle. Mark, as it turned out, had actually heard of it, and was in fact a programmer himself. Eric pulled out his phone to show Mark how the app worked, and a lively conversation ensued about all things computer. Taryn found herself listening in spite of herself, caught up in the enthusiasm Eric had as he talked. It felt so familiar— just how Wyatt had always sounded when he spoke of his work. So much competence, self-assuredness, passion for what he was doing, which had so attracted her in the beginning. And yet also the pride, the need to be right and for others to fall in line behind him, which had become so heavy as their marriage went on. Seeing the dynamic in someone else, from a distance as it were, put it all in sharp relief, and it reinforced her earlier gut reaction to Eric, to steer clear of him.

Mark asked Eric why he had come to the ranch.

Eric smirked. "Well, my shrink told me I had to take a break. I think his exact words were 'chill out.' Do something totally foreign to anything I'd ever done before. Dude ranch fits that bill for sure. Never been to Colorado so I googled and here I am."

Mark chuckled. "Can't imagine a better place to chill than here where nature is so close. Will you be going horseback riding with the rest of us tomorrow?" Dustin had announced earlier that riding lessons and a trail ride would be available first thing next morning.

"Not too sure about that. Never done it. Horses aren't really my thing." Eric's expression was a mixture of trepidation and disdain.

"Well I hope you do. Bet it would be good for you, and of course Kathy and I would love to have you come along."

Pleased, Eric agreed.

As her plate was being cleared, Taryn glanced over at Ichika, just in time to see Kaito briefly but gently stroke her hand with his finger, for the third time that evening. *Well, I think we've got us a budding romance here. Have to check that out with Paige later, see if she's picking up on it.*

Considering Paige is after Dustin too, this could be a very romantic week.

Chapter

4

While his guests were finishing breakfast the next morning, Jesse took the opportunity to make a few announcements. At 9:00 he and Dustin, and Larry if need be, would be giving riding lessons to anyone who wanted one. Then at 10:00 they would lead a trail ride.

"Who all would like a lesson?" Jesse asked.

Quickly, all three Japanese guests raised their hands. Eric did too when Taryn looked like she was going to. But she didn't. Mark chimed in that he'd like to tag along, even though he'd ridden some.

Jesse turned to Taryn and Paige. "Ladies? Care to join?" *Please say yes Taryn. I want you with me.* He'd been looking right at her when the thought hit, and he nervously cleared his throat, hoping she hadn't caught the energy of it.

Paige answered first. "Actually we've both ridden before, when we were kids. What we were hoping to do was some yoga first, then come on the trail ride. Is there a room somewhere that might work as a yoga studio?"

Jesse tried to keep the disappointment out of his voice. "Yes. In back of the spa area is an empty room that I think would do nicely. Dustin can show you where it is."

Kathy turned to Paige. "I'd love to join you, if that's okay. It's been a while since I've had a daily routine, but I used to. I might need to be reminded how to do some of the poses."

"Sure." Paige smiled. "Taryn here is an instructor and we'd be happy to have you."

Taryn broke in hastily. "Well not really an instructor. I just take over class once in a while when Patty has to be somewhere else."

Jesse tipped his hat. "Sounds like we're all set then. Ladies, if you want to come on the ride, be at the stables at ten." Relief flooded him, knowing Taryn would be near, soon.

They nodded, and Jesse left, perplexed at the intensity of his attraction. He put thoughts of Taryn aside. Many horses to get saddled.

⌒

The yoga ladies made it to the stables just in time to join the others on the trail ride. Paige immediately made a beeline to Dustin. Taryn blanched when she saw that he was wearing a holster with pistol on his hip.

Paige caught the fearful look on Taryn's face and asked, "Dustin, what's up with the gun?"

"Ah. Standard procedure when we go on rides. There are, in fact, wild animals out here in these mountains. This," he patted the gun, "is just for protection."

Paige knitted her brows in concern. "Have you ever had to use it? Is it that dangerous out there?"

Dustin chuckled. "Don't you worry darlin'. In all the time I've been here, Jesse's only shot once. And that was just to scare off a young mountain lion who hadn't yet learned not to get too close to humans. Come on, let's get you up on this horse."

Taryn looked quickly at Jesse and saw that he too had a holster and gun. For a second she had an intense experience of reactions that don't go together at all but somehow fit into the same space in her head: *oh shit, oh shit, he's got a gun, it's a gun* mixed with *oh my God, that cowboy is seriously hot*. Confused, she turned away.

Jesse had been helping Kathy on her horse and had only just turned his attention to Taryn. She was wearing the new jeans and boots she'd bought in town as well as the blue plaid shirt that set off her soft blue eyes. Her black hat seemed to bring her fully into the energy of "cowgirl" and Jesse found himself openly staring at her. Flustered, he let Larry help Taryn mount her horse, Star.

Dustin led the procession, with Paige hot on his heels. Jesse took up his position at the end of the group. He was grateful when Taryn fell into line in front of him. He'd thought this would be a time when he might talk to her, get to know her better. But suddenly he couldn't think of a thing to say, was as tongue-tied as a teenager. When she turned her head to him all he could do was nod to her.

Taryn quickly turned her head back and kicked her horse to start moving. She'd hoped to talk to Jesse, ask him about the ranch, find out more about this warm but reserved man. His cursory nod seemed to say "leave me alone" which she took as confirmation of her initial assessment of him as walled off. Her disappointment surprised her. *What does it matter? You're gone in a week—not even time to become friends, much less anything else. Which you don't want anyway*. She began to focus on the horse's movement beneath her, the majestic rocks and trees around her, and did her best to put Jesse out of her mind.

He watched as she rode along the trail in front of him. *She sits her horse well, even though she's clearly not an experienced rider.* Star stopped and put his head down, meaning to go after a particularly green bunch of grass. Taryn quickly put the reins up his neck and firmly jerked his head up. *Ah, and she knows how to take control.* Something about that last thought made his blood flame. Suddenly he was glad he hadn't started a conversation; he needed to get a grip.

How did I even get here, that I'm so out of touch with women I can't even talk to Taryn like she's a person? He thought back to the first spiritual conference he'd gone to, so many years ago, and remembered the work he'd done with his teacher during one of the morning sessions. They'd been working through the interpretation of one of his dreams, and Jesse had suddenly come face to face with the immensity of the protective shield he'd built around himself. His teacher had tried, from several angles, to get Jesse to let it down, but he'd just not been able to let himself be vulnerable again. *Why can't I let that go, even a little? I'm so drawn to Taryn; I really want to know her—who she is, what her soul is here to do on this planet. Something about her ... She feels like a flower waiting to open. Why can't I do that too? Be open, available, fully in life? I'm getting tired of being so alone ...*

Another internal voice broke in. *Remember that wicked fight? That's why. We do not want to ever go there again, ever be that hurt again. Better to stay alone, and safe. We're doing all right. Don't rock the boat.* Jesse squeezed his eyes shut, shook his head slowly, so tired of the battle. He looked up to see Taryn staring at him, her face a mixture of puzzlement and concern.

In that brief moment of unguarded helplessness, he said without thinking, "Beautiful day for self-reflection, isn't it?"

The question was so unexpected, Taryn could only blurt out,

"Yes, it certainly is," before she turned her attention to the ride again.

In spite of their yearning to talk to each other, neither was brave enough to open up, and they were mostly silent for the rest of the ride. All they could manage was to join in casual chit chat with the others from time to time.

The group arrived back at the stables just in time for lunch. One by one Dustin and Jesse helped everyone off their horses. As Dustin helped Paige dismount, taking extra care to hold onto her as long as he could without being too obvious, Jesse moved to Taryn. She dismounted gracefully, with Jesse by her side, then lost her balance when her right foot reached the ground. Instantly Jesse's strong arms were around her, supporting her. He held her close, body to body; he could feel her heartbeat. The electricity flowing between them was so strong, so sensuous, neither could move. It was only an instant to an outside observer, but to Jesse the moment was infinite, beyond time and space. Finally the word "guest" flashed through his awareness and he let her go, stepping back hastily.

"You okay?" he asked, his voice husky.

Breathlessly she answered, "Yes," and turned around so he could not see how affected she was. Gathering herself as best she could, she joined Paige and the others waiting to return to the lodge.

Dustin moved to Eric next. But Eric—always the "I can do this myself" guy—didn't wait for Dustin to assist. He flung his leg over the saddle horn and slid off. Unfortunately his heel caught in the stirrup briefly, just enough to throw him to the side, and he fell in a heap on the ground, his phone spilling out of his pocket. Spontaneously, Paige burst out laughing.

"Oh, God, Eric. I'm so sorry. That was just so cute." She made a contrite face.

Eric struggled to his feet. "Yeah well this horse riding shit is ridiculous. People have cars now. Why keep using these dumb animals—get a four-wheeler!"

He stormed off, dusting himself as he went. Paige looked after him, flabbergasted. Taryn happened to glance at Jesse, to see what he would do, and was surprised to see a hint of an amused smile curling his lips. *Ah yes, bet he's seen this before. Still, he's being very nice about it.*

Jesse turned to look directly at Taryn and smiled broadly. Then he winked, and her breath caught in her throat. She just managed to smile back before he turned to his duties tending the horses.

Paige tapped her on the shoulder and reminded Taryn they only had ten minutes till lunched would be served. They scurried off to their cabins to change.

On the way back to the main lodge they met Dustin and Jesse just coming from the stables.

"Wow, that was something else. Sparkle boy really lost it," said Paige.

"No kidding," Taryn agreed. "Quite a jerk, actually."

Jesse cleared his throat. "Well you know it's usually when we feel vulnerable that we grab onto anger as a way of trying to regain control over a situation. Anger can be very powerful, or at least can help you feel that way. So when something has you feeling embarrassed or powerless, like falling off a horse, getting angry and lashing out becomes a way to sort of destroy what made you uncomfortable. One of the ego's favorite defenses it uses to protect itself."

He glanced away, a little flustered he'd just blurted that out, then turned back to face Taryn squarely, a sudden softness filling his eyes. "You ladies have a nice lunch. And don't let Dustin talk you into helping him clean out the stalls later."

With that, he headed to the kitchen to discuss the evening meal with Bobby.

"Wow," Taryn exclaimed, looking at Dustin. "I wouldn't have expected that out of a cowboy. Is he always that profound?"

"Don't know about that. I do know that before he came to Colorado he used to go to a lot of spiritual type conferences. Maybe he got something out of it."

"Jesse, spiritual. Before he said that about Eric, I would never have guessed." She paused to reflect on what she'd observed about Jesse since she'd arrived. "But now you say that, some of what I've felt in him makes sense. He does tend to see things differently, doesn't he?"

Dustin nodded. "Yeah, and for the most part he's got a pretty good head on his shoulders. Used to be an attorney."

"Jesse, a lawyer! That's almost harder to get than him being spiritual." Taryn was fascinated. This man was a puzzle whose pieces multiplied the more she learned about him. "Keep going..."

"Well he's always been pretty closed up about his past, keeps quiet especially about his marriage. I think that ended really badly. Plus he has to always be on guard here. He's good looking, and half the women who come here want to hook up with him. That gets old after a while."

"Hummm. You're good looking too," Paige winked at him, "and you're not on guard with me at all. Or at least you don't seem to be."

Dustin gave a small shrug. "Honestly, Paige, you've been an exception. I usually keep my distance too. You just got under my skin right off the bat." He lightly touched her hand, mindful not to be too affectionate in front of the other guests. "I think it was that sassy mouth of yours," he said with a grin.

Paige blushed and smiled contentedly. Not in a long time had Taryn seen such joy on her friend's face.

Still, Taryn wanted to get back to Jesse. "If he was an attorney, how did he wind up here?"

"I think he came from Chicago. Landed in town about eight years ago after his divorce. Practiced law for a while. He knew Dan Johnson, the ranch's previous owner, from when he was a kid. Jesse bought the ranch when the old man decided to retire. That's about all I know."

Taryn got quiet then, mulling over what Dustin had said. *What would make a lawyer leave Chicago and move to Colorado, take over a dude ranch? What were these spiritual conferences he'd done? What happened to his marriage?* In spite of her established intent to remain uninvolved, she felt inexplicably drawn to know more.

They reached the lodge and the women took their places at the lunch table.

"Oh, and by the way," Dustin changed course, "the big barbecue shindig, with folks from town, will probably not be happening on our last night as advertised."

Paige pouted. "How come?"

"Heather, the woman who helps us organize it with some of the bed and breakfasts in town, was in a bad accident and will be in the hospital for at least three more days. They say she has several broken bones and was in shock when they found her. Thankfully it was nothing that won't mend, but the doctors don't want her working for two weeks. We don't really have anyone here who does that kind of event planning, so Jesse may have to cancel."

Taryn and Paige gave a knowing glance at each other, and nodded.

"Well it just so happens that Taryn and I have event planning practically in our blood. Been doing it for years for the arts council in Seattle. If Heather can talk us through the basics on the phone, I'll bet we could pick it up and give you a great barbeque."

Dustin brightened. "Seriously? That would be amazing. I'd imagine Heather could do a fifteen-minute phone call, and Jesse too. I'll tell them. Thanks, girls."

Paige pursed her lips and narrowed her eyes.

Dustin backtracked quickly. "I mean *ladies*. Will keep a lot of people from being very disappointed."

"You're very welcome, cowboy," Paige teased.

Dustin grinned at her affectionately, then announced that after they were finished with lunch, anyone who wanted to could try their hand at shooting pistols on the target range they had set up in a remote area of the ranch. Both Tadao and Kaito looked eager, as did Eric. Mark and Kathy declined.

"We've had some experience with that already. I used to hunt with my father—birds mostly. Think we'll just stay here and relax," said Mark.

Paige cast a concerned look at Taryn. Guns were not an easy subject for her friend.

Jesse came back in just as Paige was explaining this to Dustin. "Taryn here had a very bad experience involving guns." She looked at her friend questioningly. "But I'd like to try, if that's okay with you, Taryn."

Before she could answer, Jesse sat down beside Taryn and asked gently, "Would you want to talk about it?"

Surprised by the compassion in his voice, Taryn told him the story.

"We had these neighbors, seemed like a nice family. I was twelve then. The kids were early school age so it's not like I played with them. And the parents were younger than mine so the families didn't get together much. But I'd see them playing outside. Dad helping the older boy learn to ride a bike and such. I don't think anyone picked up on the warning signs. They seemed so normal."

She paused, looked at her hands dejectedly.

"One evening, just after dinner, we heard three loud bangs. My dad freaked. They were gunshots. He called the police and when they arrived the whole neighborhood was outside trying to figure out where the shots had come from. Finally everyone kind of triangulated the sounds and pointed to that family's house. When the cops went in, the husband was slumped in a chair in the living room. He was still holding the gun, but dropped it as soon as he saw them. His wife lay in a pool of blood at his feet. The kids were huddled in a bedroom, holding on to each other and crying. I didn't see any of this myself, obviously, but the description the newspapers printed is so vivid in my mind, even after all these years. And I can still hear those gunshots."

Paige reached out and put a hand on Taryn's trembling shoulder. She knew her friend had had several nightmares in college about this awful event.

When she could gather herself together again, Taryn whispered, "It just left me terrified of guns."

Softly, Jesse asked, "Would you like to lessen that fear? Maybe see what guns are really about?"

Something in his tone struck a chord with her. The energy of this quiet confident man made her feel it might be safe to come out of her overly protective shell. She would never be completely okay with guns, but she knew her fear was beyond normal, and to be able to let some of it go would be freeing.

Tentatively she said, "What did you have in mind?"

"I could show you how to handle a gun, how to shoot, let you feel the noun and verb of a gun."

"What do you mean—noun and verb?" Taryn queried, puzzled.

"Well, unless there's a human making it do something, the gun by itself is just an inert piece of metal. Noun. No more power or threat than a knife lying on a table, or a baseball bat standing in the corner of a closet. Unrealized potential so to speak." He paused, to see if she was still with him on this.

"So then the verb is when a human uses it, makes it act?" she said.

"You've got it." He added carefully, "Would you like to experience a gun, for what it is? And isn't?"

His approach felt grounded in simplicity. An offering of "just the facts, ma'am." She found herself receptive, if still a bit wary. "Okay, I'll give it a shot." Suddenly aware of what she'd just said, she laughed nervously.

Jesse smiled. "That's great, Taryn. Humor will actually go a long way to dispersing your fears." Then speaking to all those who'd signed up, "How about we meet in one hour on the porch. Be sure to bring a hat." He stood up and started toward the door.

Dustin had turned to Paige now. "So darlin', what say we mosey down to your cabin, check out that broken light bulb you were telling me about." He grinned as he said this and Paige took up the ruse.

"Oh, yeah, I'd be really grateful if you could take care of that for me."

They left Taryn alone at the table, still nervously sipping her coffee and deep in thought about Jesse.

Chapter

5

As she approached the porch, and the others waiting for the lesson with pistols, Taryn felt the tension rising to near terror levels. Only the sight of Jesse—assured, strong, looking right at her with calm steadiness—kept her from turning back.

Gently, he said, "I'm so glad you decided to try this, Taryn."

"I am too, Jesse. I'm depending on you here, you know." She realized with surprise that she trusted him, and that she was choosing to follow instead of following by default, as she had in her marriage.

Reassuringly, he offered his arm and she took it, let him lead her to the small shooting range set up on the ranch.

When they reached the shooting lanes, Taryn saw the others were already there. Eric was off to the side, busily texting on his phone as usual. As soon as he caught sight of Taryn though, Eric walked up and tried to position himself by her. Jesse motioned to Larry, the ranch hand who would be instructing today.

"Eric, I'd like you to work with Larry. I'll be helping Taryn exclusively, as she's really new to this." Jesse's tone of authority left no room for resistance.

Eric, not used to taking orders from others, narrowed his eyes and started to say something, but thought better of it and moved away with Larry. Taryn breathed a sigh of relief.

Jesse turned to Taryn, focusing his full attention on her. He knew from experience that people who'd never actually held, much less shot, a gun before could easily get caught up in the culture of negativity surrounding guns. He'd been there himself when he was younger. So he would need to tread carefully here.

He led her to the table already set up with a .22 pistol and a box of ammo. Lightly he put a hand on her arm.

"Are you ready?" he asked respectfully. He picked up the pistol and checked to be sure it wasn't loaded.

Slowly she nodded. Seeing the gun so close, the memories suddenly flooded her awareness and the fear welled up inside. She fought hard to hold it back, determined to somehow overcome it. Her hands were shaking. Finally she remembered her yoga training and took several slow deep breaths. Her body relaxed. She fixed her eyes on the pistol as Jesse moved it around in his hands, then held it out to her.

Taryn stared at it for some time, then tentatively reached out and touched the gun. It took all of her strength to just feel the cold metal, and run her fingers over the barrel, barely touching. Jesse was explaining the various parts of the pistol, the function of each, how they all worked together. He kept his voice soothing. Still, most of his words didn't fully register in her mind, overshadowed by *oh my God, I'm touching a gun*. She broke out of the trance and her eyes widened when he asked softly, "Do you think you could hold it now?"

She lifted her eyes to meet his. She'd heard somewhere that the eyes are the gateway to the soul, and in his she read a quiet confidence, a patient support, and she knew she would be safe with him. Slowly she took the gun from his hand.

Its heaviness surprised her. She supposed it shouldn't have, considering how much a hunk of metal that size should weigh. "Hunk of metal." The implications of that phrase reduced her fear—this thing was made from stuff from the earth, the way a shovel or a wrought-iron fence would be. She bounced it up and down a bit, to feel its weight. Her fingers moved to explore the barrel, the trigger, and she slowly turned the cylinder. When she looked up, Jesse was smiling at her.

"Can you feel now what I mean by the 'noun' of a gun?"

In wonder, Taryn nodded. *It really is just a thing, by itself. Just lying there, doing nothing.*

He continued. "Let me know when you think you might be ready to experience the 'verb.'"

Jesse watched as she moved her hands over the pistol, being careful to keep her finger off the trigger as he had warned. That was the first thing he taught people new to guns—never put your finger on the trigger until you're really ready to shoot. He was in awe of how quickly she'd shifted from the trembling fear to this open desire to learn. Unbidden, his admiration deepened into a yearning to know her, to be with her.

After a few minutes, Taryn looked at him bravely. "Okay, I think I could do it now. But I need to see you shoot first, see how this all works."

"Of course, Taryn. I need to show you the correct stance anyway, hand positions and so on."

He spent several minutes demonstrating how to be safe with the gun. Finally he pointed at the target and shot a bullseye.

The sound, loud even through her protective earmuffs, threw her into a panic. Again that horrible night came rushing back and she let out a cry, her eyes filling with tears. Instantly Jesse was at her side, holding her shoulders firmly, tenderly, until she could recover. When she stopped shaking, he lifted her chin, inviting her to look into his calmly intent eyes.

"Taryn, you don't have to do this. We can stop here if it's too much for you."

Gradually her fear gave way to the steadying confidence of this man. No words passed between them. It was a transfer of energy, his composure flowing into her. Slowly she shook her head.

He let go of her and once again picked up the pistol. Then he turned to her to see how she was doing. She gave him a thin smile and reached out for it.

As she settled the gun in her hand—finger along the frame just under the barrel as he'd commanded—and raised it up toward the target, she began to feel the power. She focused on the little circle on the paper hanging on a bale of hay, willing the bullet to go right to it. Her body was already anticipating the explosion that was to come when she would make the choice to squeeze the trigger. In spite of herself, and the fears she'd harbored for so long, the feeling was exhilarating. Jesse stood closely behind her, and when he put his hands on her shoulders to steady her, the jolt of passion—for life, for him—sent chills through her.

"Now set your sight, and squeeze."

She was surprised how the gun threw her back a bit even though Jesse had warned her about the recoil. Suddenly she felt her body pressed against his, and the pure sensuality of the power of the gun and the power of the man behind her gave her an adrenaline rush like nothing she'd ever experienced before. Never in her life had she smoked, but she pictured herself smoking a cigarette, like people in the movies do after sex. Inexplicably she found herself laughing out loud.

Reluctantly he stepped back from her. "Well, Taryn. That wasn't the reaction I was expecting from you! How do you feel?"

Sheepishly, she told him about wanting a cigarette and he laughed with her.

"You know I've had people say that before. It's quite the rush isn't it?"

"No kidding," she said in amazement. "Can I do it again?"

"Sure. That's what we're here for. Just cock the gun and repeat. Do you see where you hit the target by the way? Pretty good for the first time."

Taryn shot several more rounds, each time a little more comfortable with the power and intensity of the "hunk of metal" in her hand. She began to feel, down to every cell in her body, that it was her intent and action alone that made a bullet leave the gun. Finally she unloaded the remaining bullets as Jesse had shown her and handed the gun back to him.

"Thank you, Jesse. Honestly, I'm in shock. I had no idea ..." Her eyes glistened.

"Taryn, you did wonderfully. I think this was an important experience for you."

Taryn nodded through her tears.

"It so was. That feeling I had that guns are somehow 'innately evil' has faded. I think I can approach it all more rationally now, instead of through all that crippling fear." She looked askance at him and raised her eyebrows. "You know though, this doesn't change how I feel about gun control."

"Taryn, I wasn't interested in making you change your mind about anything. That was never my purpose. I was never around guns growing up, was pretty wary of them myself, so I get where you're coming from. I just wanted you to be able, after a real experience with them, to see guns for what they are, without all the *stuff* people throw on them. Do you know what I mean?"

"I do, Jesse. It really does make a difference. Has made a difference. And thank you for not trying to convince me to take a different view of guns." She sighed, shoulders sagging. "I'm wiped. Can we head back now?"

Hating that this time, this closeness between them, was ended yet knowing that she needed to rest after all she'd been through, he said simply, "Of course."

Taryn wound her way to the lodge's kitchen. After the intensity of the shooting, the swirl of emotions from the memory of her neighbor's murder, and the tantalizing physical closeness of Jesse, she desperately needed something simple and relaxing to do. She thought getting some carrots for the horses would fit that bill nicely.

As she walked down the path bordered by yellow and purple wild flowers, she reflected on the contrast between Jesse and her ex-husband. *Wyatt would never have let the opportunity to insist his ideas were the right ones pass by. It was always a given that I had to believe as he did. God it was so stifling. Jesse just let me have my own opinion. He didn't even want to change my mind.* She felt the chills run through her as the realization sank in. *He respected me, actually respected me.* Her gratitude for the cowboy and the gift he'd given her multiplied.

Bobby was in his office when she arrived. She was just going to peek her head in the door and ask about the carrots, when it occurred to her that maybe she could find out more about him as well.

"Bobby? Can I ask? How in the world did you wind up here?"

He burst out laughing.

"You mean what's this Jamaican dude doing here in Colorado, on a ranch? Well darlin', it's like this. I came to the U.S. intent on making it to Seattle. I have a friend there who said I could work for him. So I bought an old car in Florida with the little money I had and headed out. Got as far as five miles from here and the damn thing broke down. I caught a ride into town with one of the locals. And I'm sittin' in the diner, wondering what am I gonna do. I got no money left to fix the stupid car. The poor waitress is getting an earful from me when this guy in a booth comes over and starts talking to me."

"I'm guessing that was Jesse?"

"Ya. He's asking all these questions—where I'm from, where I'm going, what line of work am I in. The waitress comes over and puts my check on the table and he picks it up, tells her to put it on his tab. He was just as nice as you please."

"That sounds like Jesse." Taryn pictured the scene—Jesse reaching out to this stranger, patiently listening to his story.

"Then he blew me away. Offered me a job right there on the spot. Said he had a ranch in need of a chef and could I come take it on for a while, until I had enough money to fix the car and continue on to Seattle. Well I can tell you I didn't need much coaxing. He was a gift from heaven, Jesse was."

"That's so great." Taryn's admiration for Jesse swelled.

"Guess you can kind of figure out the rest. I never left. Jesse is such a great boss, I decided this was home. He's quiet, very respectful, and we hit it off. I asked him once why did he come over to me in that diner and he said he just had a feeling. That's Jesse. He's intuitive, as I bet you can tell."

Bobby paused and looked at Taryn thoughtfully.

"As great as Jesse was when I met him, there was always this heavy sadness around him. He mostly hid it well, but sometimes he would talk to me and I could tell something was still eating him from his life before he got here. He'd told me about having come to the ranch as a kid after his dad died. Some construction accident I think. And how Dan—that's the guy who owned this place before—he took care of him, taught him all about the ranch and hard work. It helped Jesse a lot because his mother had remarried and her focus was all on the new husband. Jesse spent most of his summers here."

"Must have been really hard on him, being second place with his mom," Taryn mused. "It's interesting he told you all that, as private as he is."

"He told me a lot of stuff he never told anyone else. I'm easy to talk to." Bobby said with a laugh.

"You are indeed," Taryn agreed. "So how did he get to be a lawyer? I have to admit, seeing Jesse the way he is now I can't imagine him as a Chicago attorney."

"He didn't say a lot about that. Just that there was a friend of his dad's who was an attorney and Jesse could see how powerful he was. Guess Jesse wanted that too."

"I can see that," Taryn mused. "What did he tell you about his marriage? His divorce?"

"Not much. I know it was bad, the breakup. But he kept that one to himself..."

Bobby dropped his eyes, and Taryn sensed that was all he wanted to say about Jesse. So she did what she'd come here to do—ask for carrots—and got up to leave.

"Thanks for taking the time to talk to me, Bobby. It's been really nice." She smiled warmly.

"It has, Taryn," he said with a grin. "Gotta get back to work now, though. Don't want the boss to see me slacking."

Taryn chuckled as she walked out the door.

She'd just turned the corner and entered the barn when she stopped short. Kaito and Ichika were not ten feet from her, in a passionate embrace.

Taryn froze. Her first impulse was to walk away quietly, but that option was gone—Ichika had just caught a glimpse of Taryn and was hastily pulling away from Kaito.

"I'm so sorry. I didn't mean to interrupt," Taryn said softly.

It was clear Kaito and Ichika had no idea what to do. They'd been found out and were embarrassed. Kaito gave Ichika an apologetic bow, and quickly left.

Taryn was appalled. "Ichika, Paige and I have thought for a while that you two were seeing each other. We think it's wonderful. I wish you wouldn't try to hide it."

"You knew?" Ichika was surprised. She thought she and Kaito had been so careful. "Our company has a strict rule about no involvement with co-workers. Tadao knows, but if anyone else discovers our secret we could both be terminated."

"Well your secret is safe here. What happens at the ranch stays at the ranch. None of us would say anything. Why would we? I think you should be open about it. Enjoy yourselves while you're here. I know I would be quite happy to watch a couple being in love, and I know Paige would too. And we can tell the others it needs to not leave here." Suddenly Taryn was envious of Ichika's situation, being so in love.

The relief and joy on Ichika's face was heartwarming. "Thank you. It really would be wonderful to act naturally, not be so afraid all the time. Will you talk to everyone, to be sure it is okay?"

"Of course I will. And I'll let you know when I have their oaths, sworn in blood."

Ichika looked horrified.

Taryn reached out to touch Ichika's arm reassuringly. "Sorry Ichika. That's just an American expression. Not to be taken literally."

Ichika brightened. "Oh. Thank you, Taryn." She bowed her head.

"Now go, go tell Kaito. And enjoy your time together."

Before they sat down for dinner at 6:00, Taryn caught Kathy and Mark, then Eric, to tell them about Ichika and Kaito. All quickly agreed to keep their relationship quiet.

"Who would we tell anyway?" Eric said with an edge in his voice. "Like we're going to call Japan and make an announcement." He looked briefly but pointedly at Taryn. "At least someone's getting lucky this week."

Taryn's eyes narrowed, and she started to voice a sharp retort. But she held back. "Well I was thinking about people in town, people who will come to the barbecue on our last night here."

Kathy was all smiles. "I thought I'd caught those vibes between them. I can't think of anything that would make me happier than to support them, give them a chance to experience their love in the open." When Ichika and Kaito entered the room she quickly walked over. Eyes twinkling, she took hold of their hands and put them together.

"We're all so happy for you. Please don't be afraid to show your love while you're here."

Ichika dropped her head. When she looked up, she was smiling shyly through misty eyes. As she turned to Kaito, he lifted her hand

and held it to his lips. They moved to the table and sat down side by side, still holding hands.

Taryn raised her glass. "To Ichika and Kaito."

The clinking of glasses brought smiles all around.

The ranch guests met again at 7:30, and all piled in the ranch vans, for their night on the town. Normally Dustin would have taken the night off, let Jim drive, but he wasn't about to miss the chance to twirl Paige around the dance floor. He knew dancing with guests was encouraged—to be sure they had a good time—as long as it didn't get too close.

Paige sat in front, giggling with anticipation, while Taryn, Kathy and Mark sat in back talking about the Seattle art scene. Jesse drove the other van and got an earful from Eric about the Sparkle app. Ichika and Kaito cuddled in the middle seat while Tadao lounged in back, watching the Rocky Mountains roll by.

The bar wasn't much for looks. None of the old-time charm of the one near the airport where Dustin had taken them the day of their arrival. The building dated to the fifties, of nineteen hundred, and was intended to be functional. Plain wood floors were surrounded by plain dry wall, with dark red paint quite a bit the worse for the wear. A stage sat at one end of the room with a small dance area in front, and pool tables hugged the other end. The bar itself ran along the far side, opposite the door. In between were tables and chairs in a mish mash of styles and ages. While the space itself was nondescript, the energy of the place was alive and kicking. As soon as Taryn walked in the front door, she already felt like she was having a good time, caught up in the rhythm of the band's music.

Everyone found tables and sat down to order the first of many rounds, but when the drinks had been ordered Taryn realized Jesse was no longer there. She scanned the room quickly, pretending to be taking it all in but secretly searching for him. Moving closer to the stage, she had a full view of the whole place but still she couldn't see him. The band started playing again and she turned to watch them. She gasped.

There he was, on stage, guitar in hand and a microphone in front of him. And he looked like he belonged there. He was dressed all in black—jeans, fancy shirt, inlayed boots and hat with silver studs in the hatband that sparkled in the stage lighting. When he started singing, his voice was deep and sensual. In spite of herself, Taryn swooned. Her head shouted "No!" but her body responded to him completely, a warmth starting deep in her pelvis and spreading through every part of her. She watched his hands as he played, his fingertips softly pushing down the strings, each finger in confident control of which note to play next. *Oh, those fingers can just touch me anytime, anywhere.* His eyes caught hers just as he was singing "no one like you" and she felt a connection so profound it seemed to transcend time and space. She stopped breathing, transfixed. When he moved his gaze, she trembled.

Eric came up then and broke the spell.

"Come on darlin', let's dance," he said as he grabbed her hand, forcing her from the chair, and spun her around.

Then he pulled her to him, too tightly for Taryn's comfort. *God what is it going to take to get through to this guy that I'm not interested.* She pushed him off just a little and made casual remarks about the band to keep Eric from trying to get too close again. When the song ended, a feisty young cowboy broke in and asked to dance with her. Gratefully, she said yes and left Eric standing alone.

The man whisked her onto the dance floor and introduced himself. "I'm John."

"Nice to meet you, John. I'm Taryn." She was having trouble focusing on her new dance partner; she wanted to concentrate on Jesse. "I'm staying at J's River Ranch for a week. Where are you from?"

"I live here in town, have my whole life. Native Coloradoan." He twirled her around and led her closer to the back of the room, farther away from the stage. To Taryn's immense relief, a young woman tapped her on the shoulder, asking to cut in. She clearly knew John well, as she immediately wrapped her arms around him and snuggled into his neck. They danced away.

While Taryn surreptitiously watched, Jesse played several songs with the band, then left the stage with them at break time. Dustin and Paige joined her.

"Jesse can really play, can't he?" she said to Dustin.

"Yeah, he can. He's not a permanent member of the band, as such, but they like him to play with them now and again. He just does it for fun."

Dustin turned to say something to John, who was passing by on his way to the bar.

"He's really hot on stage, isn't he?" Paige whispered to Taryn with a sly smile. Dustin, barely hearing her question, seemed not to notice the undertone of Paige's remark. Taryn blushed but decided not to respond to Paige's teasing. Instead she pointed to the line dancers just getting started on another song the interim DJ was playing and remarked, "Aren't Ichika and Kaito cute doing the cowboy hustle? They're really catching on quick. Don't imagine this is something they do in Japan much."

"And there's Kathy and Mark too. They've obviously done this before—they're pros," Paige exclaimed with admiration. "Let's get in."

She grabbed Taryn's hand and they slipped into the line. The particular dance everyone was doing now was new to them but since they'd taken a few line dancing classes at the gym it didn't take long for them to figure out the steps. Dustin joined them after a bit and Paige was on cloud nine. Eric took up his preferred position at Taryn's side and followed along as well as he could. He was trying hard to learn, and was laughing so much, Taryn found herself enjoying his company. When the song ended, she gave him a high five. Another song began, this time for a dance Taryn and Paige knew well. Eric had caught the patterns of the first dance and actually picked this one up quickly. Taryn was impressed.

When the song ended she turned to him. "You did really well, Eric. That was a lot of fun."

"Thanks," Eric said, surprised at how friendly she was being. The DJ had put on a slower song now, and politely he asked, "Would you like to dance?"

She smiled warmly. "I would, Eric, but I think I need a breather. I'm going to sit for a minute. Maybe later," she said and moved away.

She sat down at a table to the side of the dance floor and watched as Dustin and Paige danced, cheek to cheek. Taryn was delighted to see her friend having so much fun. John came up again then and pulled her up, twirled her into his arms. As she fell against him, she caught sight of Jesse. He was watching her with a look she could only interpret as sadness. Puzzled, she pushed John to a more comfortable distance while they danced. She tried hard to hear what he was saying to her, making small talk, but that look from Jesse consumed her thoughts.

There was a short break in the music as the DJ left the stage so the band could get set up again. Kathy decided to take the opportunity to talk—without having to shout—to Paige. She had to pry her away from Dustin, then asked, "Hey, what's up with Taryn? She was pretty friendly with Eric while they were line dancing. I thought she didn't like him."

Paige replied, "I wouldn't say Taryn doesn't like Eric. She doesn't want to be involved with him, or anyone, right now. And he's so insistent, she kind of has to shake him off. He was all over her the minute we picked him up at the airport."

"Yeah, I've seen that too." She paused. "I'd say Jesse is interested in her too. Have you seen the looks he gives her?"

Paige agreed but was uncertain how much Taryn would want her to say, so she just nodded. The band began playing and she was relieved when Dustin came back up to dance again.

His second set with the band finished, Jesse stood alone at the bar for a moment. He was astounded by his reaction to seeing Taryn dance with other men. Emotions he'd not let himself feel for years welled up in him. His pulse quickened as he watched Taryn's hips swaying sensually to the music. He heard her laugh at something Eric said and wished it had been his words that had brought her joy. He cringed when John pulled her in close. That was where he so wanted to be. Relief washed through him as the song ended and John left her side. Impulsively, Jesse walked up to Taryn and asked her to dance.

"Can't leave one of our guests unattended," he said awkwardly, his voice husky.

It was a slow song and Taryn's heart pounded as Jesse took her into his arms. He intentionally held her half a breath away, not wanting to break the host-guest distance that protected him from completely falling for her. Still the air vibrated between them.

She felt his gentle hand on the small of her back, remembered his fingers playing the strings of his guitar, and felt desire building. *Oh, no.* She could not resist though, and slowly she let herself melt into Jesse until her head was resting on his shoulder, her cheek against his.

As they moved across the floor, he smelled her hair, felt her breasts brush his chest. There was no way he could deny how much he wanted her. To be with her, to know her, let her know him. And he hadn't let himself want a woman for so long. She felt so good, so right in his arms. When the song ended, he let go of her reluctantly when she lifted her head and looked at him. Her eyes were filled with a question he wasn't ready to answer.

Eric came bounding up then and ripped her away. Taryn tried to pull back, turned to Jesse, but he had moved away, embarrassed he had been so obvious about his desire to be close to her. In desperation, she told Eric she needed a bathroom break and bolted.

Oh God, what are you doing? You can't be letting yourself get hung up on this man. He's made it so clear he doesn't want to be involved with anyone. Dustin said so. And he has his pick of all these women who come to his ranch. What makes you think he would really want you?

She made it to a bathroom stall and locked herself inside. *But he held me so close, felt so totally with me while we danced. The way he touched me—it didn't feel casual.* She stopped thinking and just let herself feel what it had been like to dance with him. Body to body, her breasts pressed to his chest, his hand on her back, thighs brushing and his warm cheek resting against hers. Her body was still buzzing from the contact, the physical closeness of a man, the desires she had let slip away from her life. Abruptly her head broke in. *Jeez honey you have got to stop this. He does not want you. He was just—what did he say?—not leaving a guest unattended. Go find John and have some harmless fun. You're on vacation, not looking for a man, so act like it.*

Taryn and Jesse avoided each other for a while, dancing with others. She watched as he moved with a woman from town, one he clearly knew well, trying to get a sense of just how close they really were. *What the hell girl, are you actually being jealous here?* He watched as John pulled Taryn closer and closer while they danced, and winced. Both fought the feelings that could not be ignored.

Mark and Kathy broke the tension by being the first to ask to return to the ranch. Jesse had told everyone earlier that he would be taking the early van back while others could party till the bar closed down. Taryn impulsively said she'd like to go too, before she'd had time to realize how hard it would be to be in the van with him now. Luckily Mark slid in the front seat with the women in the back, Taryn behind Jesse.

For a while they all chatted about the bar, the line dancing, how cute Ichika, Kaito and Tadao had been learning the steps. But it wasn't long before even Mark and Kathy felt the intensity of the energy passing between Jesse and Taryn, and everyone fell silent for the rest of the drive.

Chapter

6

At breakfast the next morning the talk was all about country dancing and hangovers. Kaito and Tadao, and Eric of course, had decided to really cut loose and they were suffering for it today. Eric seemed unable to engage in conversation; he just sat texting on his phone. Ichika had not overindulged in the drinking like the guys, and chatted excitedly about the line dancing with Taryn and Paige She'd never tried it before and was now hooked. She'd already ordered several DVDs online so she could teach her friends back home.

They were just finishing their ranch-sized meals of eggs, bacon, French toast and fried potatoes when Jesse and Dustin walked in to discuss plans for the morning.

Dustin spoke first. "So on the schedule is a trail ride, led by Jesse and me, probably up the north ridge. How many of you will be going?"

Tadao, Kaito and Eric mumbled something unintelligible and continued slowly sipping their coffee.

"I'd like to go. Be good to get some cool fresh air after being in the bar." Taryn looked at Jesse as she said this, and he dropped his eyes to the floor, not sure if he wanted to know what she meant by that.

Ichika shook her head and said, "I'm still exhausted from last night. My plan is to read until I fall asleep, which will not be long."

Mark threw his arm around Kathy and pulled her close. He explained, "We've got a couples massage booked at ten. We'll catch up with you all later."

Paige was about to say she'd go on the ride too when it hit her that this would be a perfect time for Taryn and Jesse to have some time to themselves. She'd been watching her friend struggle with her attraction to the handsome cowboy. In spite of Taryn's protestations to the contrary, Paige knew Taryn was falling for Jesse, and this was a good thing. *Girl needs some action*. So she echoed the others.

"I think I'll pass. Maybe I'll join you at the spa," she said, turning to Mark and Kathy. When she saw their dismayed expressions, she quickly added, "Well not *join* you, but do the massage and hot tub thing as well."

Kathy laughed. "Good plan."

"Well then," said Dustin, giving a quick glance at Paige. "Looks like it's just Taryn then so Jesse can take her and I can get some other things done around here. That okay with you, boss?" Jesse nodded, so Dustin asked, "What time do you guys want to get going?"

"How about 9:30? Does that work for you Taryn?" Jesse asked. He struggled to keep his voice even, felt the excitement of soon being with her rising in him.

"You got it. At the stables?" Taryn's heart raced.

Jesse nodded again. He tipped his hat and left, along with Dustin.

Paige smiled, eyes sparkling.

Back at her cabin, Taryn was just about changed for the trail ride when Paige burst through her door.

"Derek's been in an accident. They can't tell me yet how badly he's hurt ..." She broke down then and started crying. Taryn reached out to hold her.

"Oh my God, Paige, that's awful. I'm so sorry. How did you find out?"

"The hospital just called. I was still at the lodge and Jesse and Dustin were there and ..."

Her body shook with the sobs, leaving no breath for continuing. Finally she said, "They've arranged a private jet to pick me up at the local airport. It should be here in about thirty minutes. I have to go ..." She looked frantic, and unsure of what to do next.

"Do you want me to come with you? For support?" Taryn added lamely, "I'm sure he'll be okay."

"Yes. No." A hint of Paige's level headedness showed up. "I really don't know what you could do. Stay here for now. They said he was in surgery, so it will be a while before they can tell me more. I'll let you know when I get to the hospital." Then she broke again and in a plaintive voice said, "If it's really bad I might ask you to come home."

"Of course I will. Anything you need. Just tell me."

"I've gotta go." Paige gave her friend a quick hug and dashed out.

"I hope he's all right. I'm here for you, girlfriend," Taryn called after her.

By the time Taryn got to the stables, Jesse had Lucky and Star saddled up and ready to head out on the trail. As he had on the first ride, he had on a holster and gun. Taryn glanced at them and marveled at the mildness of her reaction. So much of the fear she'd had about guns had dissipated in her experience of shooting one herself. She almost smiled, but then remembered the situation at hand.

"Jesse, I'm not sure I can go on this ride. Paige's son has been in an accident ... oh, you know that already. I think I need to stay here, to be here for Paige."

The jolt of dashed hope he felt was a shock to him. Recovering slightly, he said, "Dustin has already taken her to the airport. She has at least a two-hour plane ride, then however long it takes through Seattle traffic to get to the hospital. We should be back in plenty of time for you to get her call when she has more to tell you. But it's up to you."

Taryn relented. "You're right. There's nothing to be done now. Better to be out doing something than sitting around dwelling on it. God I hope Derek's okay. He's Paige's pride and joy. I don't know what she'd do ..." Tears welled in her eyes, ran down her cheeks.

Without thinking, Jesse reached out to gently wipe away a tear, then quickly withdrew his hand. *Too forward. She's a guest, remember.*

To his relief, Taryn seemed to have taken the gesture as nothing more than a sign of concern for her situation and said simply, "Let's get going then."

They wound up the side of the hill just behind her and Paige's cabins, Jesse in front and Taryn behind. The clomping of the horses, the cool clean air, and the beauty of the Colorado mountains gradually soothed Taryn's nerves. She let Derek go, temporarily, knowing whatever action might be called for from her would come later. She even pushed away the memories of her dance with Jesse the night before, let herself settle into just following the cowboy on the horse in front of her.

Until the trail widened enough for them to ride side by side, and the horses quickened into an easy canter. Neither Taryn nor Jesse could deny then how natural they were as a pair, so in sync, so connected. Both felt it. At the same moment they looked into each other's eyes and smiled.

When they reached a small stream and stopped to let the horses drink, Jesse looked up at the sky and frowned. Intuition told him those clouds coming in were more than just harmless cumulus, but he chose to ignore the threat. He didn't want to cut short his time with Taryn. In spite of himself, he felt so comfortable with her. Like having a warm blanket around his shoulders. Like discovering the wall he'd built around himself actually did have a window in it.

He'd not felt that way with his ex-wife, Veronica, he realized. She was more the dazzling sort, who'd tease and keep you just slightly off center. Life with her had been exhilarating at first, all that attention from the boss's daughter. Went to his head, heads, both of them. Now, experiencing the difference between how he felt around Taryn and how he'd felt with Veronica, he could see what an impossibly crazy farce his marriage had been.

"How are you doing, Taryn? Getting tired of the riding yet?"

"No way, Jesse. This is wonderful, just what I needed. Do you have things you have to do back at the ranch? We can head back if you want." She couldn't hide the disappointment in her voice at the thought this could end soon.

"Actually I was thinking I'd like to show you something, a waterfall. It's not too far from here. Should add a half hour or so to our ride."

She brightened. "I'm game. Come on Star, let's go."

They'd just reached the top of the hill, and Jesse was finally unable to ignore how ominous the dark clouds beginning to close in on them were, when his phone rang.

"Hello? Hello? Is that you, Dustin? I'm not hearing you very well."

"Yeah. Hey Jes ... That storm ... was supposed to go north ... way south. They're ... a lot of snow. Where ... you guys?"

"Damn. We're a good hour from the ranch. I took Taryn up to the waterfall. And just as we're speaking the first flakes are coming down. I don't think we'll make it back."

"Did you say ... snowing? Maybe ... hunters' cabin ..."

"You're right. We'll head for the hunters' cabin. Call you when I can."

"Good ... b ..."

Jesse glanced again at the sky, which was full with snow ready to fall, then turned to Taryn.

"Dustin says the storm is coming our way. The weather reports had said yesterday that it would be a big one but stay north of here. We're really not going to make it back to the ranch. There's a hunters' cabin about a half mile from here. It's kept pretty well stocked. We can wait out the storm there."

Taryn looked up at the sky, which was becoming darker with each passing moment. The first snowflakes fell on her cheeks and began to stick on her hair.

"Okay. Any kind of shelter is fine with me. It's getting serious, and cold."

"No kidding. Follow me." Jesse gave Lucky a hard kick and went galloping down the ridge with Taryn close behind.

When the cabin came into view, Taryn—wet and shivering—decided it was just about the most wonderful thing she had ever seen.

While the log cabin itself was small, there was also a lean-to on the side that would shelter the horses. They dismounted quickly and pulled off the saddles. After rubbing down Star and Lucky, they covered them with blankets and Jesse filled the bucket with water from the pump nearby. Then he hustled Taryn into the cabin.

It was actually more spacious inside than she would have guessed. And while everything from the walls to the furniture to the floor was quite rustic, there was a functional kitchen, a tiny bathroom and a large fireplace for heat. Sliding curtains offered privacy for the two bedroom areas. And—oh wonderful—there were many blankets.

Jesse commanded, "You'll need to get those wet clothes off right away. All of them."

Her look of shock bordering on fear nearly made him burst out laughing.

"Keeping wet clothes on will drain your body heat, Taryn. Wrap up in the blankets. I'm going back out for firewood."

Her teeth were chattering but she managed an "okay."

She grabbed two thick quilts and went into the bathroom to change. She wrung out her wet jeans, jacket, shirt and underwear as best as she could, then hung them over the shower door to dry. By the time she was out, Jesse was in the process of building a large fire in the fireplace. She gratefully sat down cross legged on the couch in front of it, with the quilts wrapped around her. Jesse quickly got some water boiling for coffee in the kitchen, then he too found a large blanket and got out of his clothes. With the blanket draped over one shoulder and under the other arm to leave it free, he brought two steaming cups of coffee to the sofa and offered one to her.

"Thank you, Jesse," said Taryn as she took the cup from his hands and sipped. The hot liquid warmed her inside, and she began to relax.

Jesse sat down on the couch, at the other end. He had brought his phone as well, thinking to call Dustin and let him know they were okay. But as he'd expected, the call wouldn't go through.

"We'll have to wait till it stops snowing, try again when it clears. Guess we're stuck here for a while."

"I'm just happy to be inside, and warm." She smiled. "Any idea how long this storm will last?"

"Well it wasn't supposed to get this far south, according to the reports I saw last night. Otherwise I would never have started this long trail ride. I think it's a pretty big one, but who knows. It's already not what anyone expected."

Suddenly the reality of their situation was inescapable—the possibility of an extended stay in this cabin, just the two of them, alone. Previous thoughts of their attraction to each other brought on an awkward silence. Awareness that there was nothing between their bare bodies except a couple of blankets was terrifying, yet exciting too. And neither knew what to do about it.

Finally Jesse said nervously, "So what was it that brought you and Paige to J's River Ranch?"

Thank God, something easy to chat about. The tension left Taryn's shoulders.

"Well, Paige is involved with the arts council in Seattle, and at their annual fundraising auction she bid on this week for two here. I guess she thought it might be a good distraction for me; I'm coming up on three years since my ... divorce. She didn't really think she would win it but, here we are."

"Well I'm really glad she did," Jesse blurted out before he could think. Quickly he added, "Seems like you're having a good time."

"We are."

Again there was an awkward silence. *Jeez, why am I suddenly afraid to talk to this guy? I've already settled this—nothing is going to happen with him. I don't even want that.* But the tinglings deep inside her said otherwise. She tried her best to ignore them.

Jesse got up hastily, poked at the fire which hadn't needed tending. *Oh God, what do I do now?*

Jesse sat back down and took a sip of his coffee. At a loss for what to say, he suddenly jumped to his feet again.

"I think I saw some protein bars in the cupboard when I was looking for the coffee. Would you want one? We could call it lunch," he said lamely.

"Uh, sure." She was having a hard time reading him now. In the short time she'd known him he'd been so confident and serene. His current lack of composure was unsettling, and added greatly to her own uneasiness.

While he walked back to the kitchen, Jesse tried to calm down.

Get a grip man. You're acting like you did in middle school. You're a person; she's a person. Not only that, she's your guest. Get back into host mode and make the best of this situation by having a nice easy conversation with her.

He handed her a bar before wrapping his quilt more tightly around himself and taking his place at the other end of the couch.

"Tell me more about this arts council. You said Paige is involved. Were you?"

Inwardly, Taryn breathed a sigh of relief. *Light and breezy—I can do that.*

"Yes I was, for a while. I majored in art history in college, well that and accounting, which is what my dad insisted I study. Got to have a sensible skill, you know. But it was the art I really loved.

Working with the arts council was fun, but now I just help out with the annual art show in August. That's what I was doing just before coming here."

"And what do you do for them?" Jesse could feel the energy smoothing out again, thankfully. He unwrapped his own protein bar.

"Organizational stuff mostly. Sometimes I help put together the brochures and posters, work with the guest lists and invitations, that sort of thing. Sometimes they even hire me to do special projects like cataloging new acquisitions. During the show I usually manage the entry desks and work with the catering staff. But I had to cut that part a little short this year."

"Why's that?" Jesse asked between bites.

"I was helping my daughter, Amy, get moved into her new apartment."

"Oh, you have kids." *Don't know why it never occurred to me that she would have a family. She said she was married so it makes sense she would have had kids.* The image of her with children opened up a whole side of her he'd not yet felt.

"Well they're hardly kids anymore. Josh is about to be twenty-three, has been on his own for a couple years now. Amy is just starting her last year of college. She's moved in with two of her friends and won't be coming back home after she graduates. So I'm an empty-nester now." Her eyes misted as the full import of the words hit her, and she dropped her hands into her lap.

"That must be hard for you. I've known a lot of people who are thrilled when their kids leave home, but you seem to be the opposite. You must love them very much," Jesse said softly.

She brightened. "I do, Jesse. Being a mother was the most rewarding thing I've ever done in my life. I've pretty much loved every part of it. Watching them grow, become real human beings—they're my best friends now." Remembering herself, she quickly asked, "Do you have kids?"

"No, short marriage. My wife and I never got to that point. Probably for the best, considering." He gave her a wan smile.

A silence hung in the air. Taryn wasn't sure how to respond. His words told her clearly that there was a story there, and that he did not want to share it. She decided to completely change the subject.

"So tell me what it's like to run a dude ranch."

Jesse chuckled, grateful to her for having turned the conversation back to something lighter. He had lots of fun stories to tell her, and as he relaxed into them, his natural humor came through. Before long he had her in stitches. In fact, she almost let loose of the quilt around her when he relayed the tale of Dustin's first attempt at line dancing.

"Boy's got two left feet, I tell you. Larry was trying his best to go slow, so Dustin could repeat his moves. But Dustin kept getting it backwards. Larry would slap his foot behind him and Dustin would put his leg in front. Larry would slide to the left and Dustin to the right. Almost like he was mirroring Larry instead of matching him. You'd think he was dyslexic. Finally they both just gave up. Got pretty drunk that night if I remember right."

"Bet that would have been a great video for YouTube."

"No kidding. Dustin must have practiced on his own though, because the next time I saw him out on the dance floor he did a surprisingly good job."

"He and Paige certainly danced well the other night." Taryn smiled, remembering.

"Yes indeed. I'm sure you've already noticed how taken he is with your friend."

Taryn chuckled. "And she with him. Honestly, I haven't seen her so happy with anyone for a long time. It's kind of fun to watch."

"What's the story with her? Has she ever been married? I mean I'm guessing she's not now."

"No, she's not. Her husband died when Derek was six months old."

"Wow, that must have been difficult."

"It was, though not as much as you'd think. She just picked herself up and concentrated on raising Derek. I was amazed actually."

"Sometimes the suddenness of a death is easier to take than the slow unraveling of a relationship, where the other person is still there but not. Like a divorce."

He froze. He hadn't meant to be so blunt with that.

Taryn felt the shift in him, toward the kind of reflective thinking he'd shown when Eric got angry falling off the horse. Something about his calm demeanor—especially how he'd said the word divorce—made her want to say more, to tell him about the whole messy, painful separation from Wyatt. But she stopped herself short, certain he wouldn't want to be that personal.

He sensed strongly what she was feeling—her desire to open up, then her hesitation. He felt his own protective instincts kick in, and the fear that kept him from wanting to get closer as well. *What are you doing, bringing up such things? Didn't you learn anything from your own marriage? Stop trying to get close. You'd just get hurt again.*

Finally, uncertain as to how he should relate to her now, he said, "You know, I think I should go check on the horses. We gave them water earlier but they'll be needing food now too. Would you excuse me for a minute?"

"Of course ..." She wrapped the quilt more tightly around her shoulders, energetically withdrawing, as he had.

Hurriedly, Jesse walked out the door.

Taryn stared after him. *Good grief. What the H are we going to talk about now? He'll barely talk about himself and I've already said as much as I want to about my life. Crap.*

She got up, adjusted her quilt so she could walk, and started looking around the cabin, checking out the contents of the kitchen cabinets and drawers, just to see what was available that might keep them busy through the hours ahead. In one of them she found an old deck of cards.

Games. Maybe we could just play gin rummy or something.

Taryn carefully counted the cards, groups of four, should be thirteen of them. But the last group was short. By two. Fifty cards.

Can't play a full game of anything with an incomplete deck. Every time you'd try to make a set or a sequence, you'd always know the next card you needed might be one of the ones missing.

She stared at the deck as the realizations flooded her.

God that's just how I felt the last years of being married to Wyatt. Like I was not playing with a full deck. Like he was holding two of my cards, was controlling what I had to play with. Actually it was more like I somehow gave him those two cards, let him run the show. And I just sat there the whole time, trying to play short-handed.

The deck of cards forgotten, she walked back to the couch and plopped down.

Jesse tended to the horses, who seemed to be doing fine in their little shelter. When he'd finished with them, he started picking up wood for the fire. He worked mostly on autopilot, his mind very much on the woman inside the cabin.

I don't know how much longer I can keep this up. I know I'm supposed to be the host, keep things light. But I really do want to know her, like really. And it seemed like she might be willing ... for a minute she almost let herself go there.

He felt the heat rise.

If I'm honest with myself, I know she's not the only one who needs to be more authentic and available. Just before that fear gripped me again, I almost felt like opening up to her too.

The logs he was gathering suddenly fell to the ground again as he realized what had just happened for him. Deep inside, the scales had tipped—his desire to know Taryn, be close to Taryn, had surpassed his need to keep himself protected. He stood silent for a minute, in awe. Then picking up the logs he'd dropped, he allowed the once forbidden possibilities to emerge.

Could it be? A personal, vulnerable conversation? Do I dare?

Chapter

7

Taryn was staring at the dwindling fire and sighed heavily just as Jesse opened the door, barely covered in his quilt.

Immediately he sensed she had shifted to a deeper level while he was out. He quickly threw down the logs he'd brought in, then sat down near her and decided to take a chance.

"If you don't mind me asking, what happened to your marriage?" His voice was hesitant, but coaxing.

At first the question put her off. *That's a bit personal isn't it? I thought we were going to keep it light here.* Jesse seemed to be genuinely concerned though, so she moved past the bristly reaction and let herself surrender to the moment. At least it was something to talk about that could take her mind off the insanely hot man sitting across from her.

Smiling grimly, she said, "I guess the bottom line is he left me for another woman." She dropped her head, looked down at her hands fidgeting with the edge of her blanket.

"That must have hurt," he said compassionately.

"Yeah, no kidding. It was a good friend of ours. The affair had been going on for over a year, right in front of me. And I didn't see it." Her eyes filled with tears.

"I'm sorry, Taryn." He wanted to reach out, comfort her, but he didn't trust himself to not do more than that, wasn't at all sure she'd welcome his touch.

She shrugged. "Honestly we hadn't been that happy for a long time. You know—big shot VP and corporate wife slash homemaker. We'd definitely grown apart. I just didn't know how much. He never said he was unhappy ..."

"Guys aren't always good about saying stuff like that."

"Wasn't just him though." There was bitter resignation in her voice. "The way we'd become ... It wasn't good for me but I refused to look at things closely enough to let myself see it. Sometimes I wonder what I would have done if I'd been more honest with myself." She was surprised how easily the words were flowing, how comfortable it was to open her heart to him—this almost stranger.

"How do you mean?" He studied her, trying to feel the story behind the words.

"I don't know. Maybe talked to him. Maybe seen a counselor. But as it is—I just can't seem to get over how he cheated on me. With a friend, no less."

"Unfortunately it's a pretty common way for relationships to end, leaving for someone else."

Her face twisted with consternation and she raised her hands in a "what the F" gesture.

"Yeah but he was always so adamant about how he would never. I can't tell you how many times he would say what an awful thing that was to do to a person you'd loved. That no matter how bad things got he would never do that. One of his friends cheated on his wife and Wyatt would barely speak to him for a year. Finally the friend patched it up with his wife and things went pretty much back to normal, but Wyatt was furious with him when it happened. Then he goes and does the same damn thing, to me."

She was angry now, practically shaking with the intensity of her emotions. Her eyes flashed hot.

"Will you tell me more about how the marriage was for you? You said you'd grown apart?" Jesse said quietly.

She calmed a bit, remembering the tedium her life had become in the last years she and Wyatt were together.

"Yes. My life as corporate wife, with all the entertaining and keeping up appearances and all was fun for a while. I volunteered on the arts council with Paige and we had a good time. And of course the kids—raising them was great, like I said before. Most fulfilling thing I've ever done. But it just crept up on us, and finally I had to admit that Wyatt and I didn't have much in common anymore. It felt like I valued what he did and contributed to us, but he didn't value my contribution and really didn't have much interest in what I did in my life. We didn't talk about anything personal any more, just kids and his work and what to do with the landscaping." The sad faraway look in her eyes spoke volumes. "Finally I realized he didn't even see me anymore, and what was worse was I couldn't see myself either. I felt like a shell, when I let myself feel. Which wasn't often. I kept so busy, to keep from facing it."

She stopped, weighed down by it all, then shrugged hopelessly.

He waited patiently for her to continue.

"Of course after the divorce I did what anyone who's been dumped is supposed to do. I found the therapist everyone raved about and spent two years spilling my guts out on her lavender tufted couch but all I really got was the 'oh you just grew apart.' And then the stuff about how I was looking for a father image and he wanted a little girl, so when I grew up he had to find another little girl. Guess there was some truth in that but the problem with her theory was that the woman Wyatt left me for, Greta, is hardly the little girl. She's an accomplished independent woman, nice too. Before she hooked up with my husband, I liked her very much." She smiled weakly.

Again she stopped, certain she'd said way more than what he wanted to hear.

Carefully, he asked, "And you said the affair had been going on for a year? That you didn't see it. Are you sure?"

She'd already opened herself more than she had in a long time, surrendering to the vulnerability. Something in her decided to drop all pretense of ignorance. "Well, if I'm completely honest—which I haven't been, even with myself—I saw the signs. The looks between them, the accidental touching, the late nights he 'worked.' I guess I couldn't deal with it, so I pushed it all aside. I forbade myself from even thinking about it," she said dejectedly.

"I was sure you knew, deep down," Jesse said. "You pick up on things pretty quickly; I've seen it."

Taryn sighed heavily, and her eyes misted. She shrugged in reluctant agreement. Her quilt slid down just a bit off one shoulder and she quickly pulled it up again.

Jesse thrilled at the sight of Taryn's naked skin, but resolutely pushed the feelings aside.

"Is it possible you wanted out?" he asked softly, but pointedly.

She looked intensely into his eyes, saw the sincerity behind his query. "I don't know," she said honestly. "It's not a question I ever allowed myself to ask. Just asking would mean giving up on the fairy tale, giving up on what I thought was supposed to last forever."

"I know, giving up on a dream is a hard thing to do."

She looked so crestfallen he almost wasn't sure he should continue. But he had a sense ...

"Taryn, would you be interested in seeing this from another perspective?"

She raised her head in surprise, searched his face for a clue as to what he might mean. All she could read was his desire to help, somehow.

"Yes, I guess so," she said tentatively.

"I could be wrong, but I'm getting the feeling that deep down you wanted out, long before it finally ended. That the marriage wasn't serving you, your life, any more. You didn't say these words, but it feels like you were being drained by the relationship. Actually the lack of relationship. And part of you knew you needed out but you were clinging to the 'should' of staying. Am I off base here?"

She struggled with the full impact of his words. They forced her to see what she'd so long refused to acknowledge, and now the truth couldn't be denied any longer.

"No. If I'm really honest with myself, you're right." She glanced at the kitchen, remembering her experience with the cards. "You know, while you were feeding the horses, I was looking around and found a deck of cards. I thought maybe we could play a game or something. But when I counted, two cards were missing, and it suddenly felt like that's how I'd been with Wyatt. Like I wasn't playing with a full deck. I don't mean mentally, the way that phrase is usually used. But like I'd somehow given over two of my cards to him, leaving him with the upper hand, always. Does that make any sense?"

Jesse was relieved that she had already caught a glimpse of what the marriage had been doing to her. His voice full of compassion, he said, "It makes perfect sense."

"These past three years have been tough, no doubt about it, but in the last six months I've actually started to feel like me again. I spent so many years not even asking myself what *I* wanted that I didn't even know any more. It was all about the kids, all about Wyatt, what they would want."

Suddenly she went crimson as she remembered, and hurriedly looked away. Too late. He'd seen her expression and was clearly expecting her to speak it. *God I can't tell him this. Can I? He's being so easy to talk to. But I haven't even told Paige. Oh shit ...*

Obviously something had hit, and he waited expectantly for her to continue.

Bashfully she said, "I used to bury myself in steamy romance novels when no one else was home. A way to escape my life. Jeez, Jesse, I've never told anyone this. I don't know why I'm telling you."

She glanced quickly at him, to see how he was taking this, hoping against hope that he wasn't laughing at her. When she saw understanding in his eyes, she let a small grateful smile touch her lips.

Softly, he said, "Because it's another piece of the puzzle. You wanted out. And at least part of you would have liked to find someone new. I think that's what the romance novels were about."

Her eyes went wide as she took this in. She wanted to protest, blurt out "no I'm a good girl" but the memory of the thrills she'd gotten reading those novels stopped her. *Oh my God, is he right? The novels weren't just for fun? Did I really want someone else, someone not Wyatt?*

The shocked look on her face showed him he was on track. *My intuition was right. Funny she never saw that herself; she's obviously perceptive. I've seen it so many times, but it still blows me away how people can hold onto their stories about how their life is even though there's massive evidence to the contrary.*

"You okay?" he asked gently.

She mumbled something unintelligible, was clearly confused, and Jesse knew she needed space now. Some things take time to be absorbed.

"I'll see if I can find something to make us to eat." He rose, clutching his blanket tightly. As he walked past her to the kitchen, he touched her softly on the shoulder.

Because the hunting cabin was infrequently occupied, it was stocked with only non-perishable food items. He found some canned beef stew, canned corn and Bisquick. Taryn wasn't vegetarian, thank goodness. He'd seen her happily eating steak the evening before. He mixed up the biscuit dough, formed it into little balls with his hands and squished them into flatter disks. Into the propane oven they went while he heated the stew and corn on the propane stove. Taryn was still sitting on the couch, silent, staring at the fire, and he wondered if she would even be able to eat once the meal was ready.

Just as he was getting the biscuits out of the oven, he heard a muffled "That smells good" from her and he breathed a sigh of relief.

"I'll bring it over in just a minute," he called.

Jesse dished up the stew and corn into bowls, put the biscuits on a plate and brought everything on a tray. He'd also found a bottle of wine they might share, if she wanted.

To keep the quilt out of the way while he was cooking, he'd wrapped it around his middle, like a towel, leaving him unclothed above the waist. As he walked into the living area, the sight of his strong arms and naked chest covered in thick dark hair gave Taryn a start, and involuntarily she felt herself flame. He was smiling warmly at her, adding to her meltdown. She trembled and looked away.

He caught the brief flash of passion on her face and stood flustered for a minute, finally remembering his state of undress. Quickly he put the tray down—to not drop it—as his own desire for her overtook him.

Holy shit. Holy shit. Dude, you can't go there. Distract, something to distract. "Go ahead and start eating. I'm going to try to call out again."

Jesse hastily walked over to the desk, desperate to calm down. He picked up his phone but his intent turned to dismay when he saw there were still no bars.

"Crap. I was hoping to just let Dustin know we're okay. I'd hate to think of him sending out a search party in this weather."

Taryn recovered too, found her voice. "You know a friend once told me that sometimes you can get a text out even if there's not enough signal strength to make a call. You might give it a try."

"Humm. I'd not heard that before. But you're right; I should try." He typed in a text.

> *Made it to the cabin. We're safe, waiting out the storm.*

"Guess we wait to see if it goes through."
In just a few seconds his phone pinged.

> *Very glad to hear it. Looks to be a bad one so stay put.*

> *Will do.*

"Dustin says stay put for now," Jesse said as he looked out the window. "Damn, we've got a good six inches already and it's still really coming down."

He turned, finally able to look at Taryn with some semblance of steadiness.

"How's the stew?"

"Pretty good actually. Come have some while it's hot?" She'd steadied herself too while he played with the phone, remembered her earlier desire to keep things light.

"Sure. Want some wine?" He approached, uncertain where to sit. The couch seemed too close, considering. But the chair was too far away ... *Damn, don't go weird on her. Sit next to her like you were before. And settle down.*

She'd nodded, so he poured two glasses of wine, handed one to her. Then he grabbed the afghan draped over the back of the couch and covered his chest before sitting down.

She almost laughed out loud at the sudden disappointment, and relief, when the tantalizing view disappeared. *Oh for heaven's sake, girl, come back to earth. Even if you wanted this to go somewhere, there's no sign he does.*

"Thanks, Jesse."

"Sorry there's no butter or jam for the biscuits. Only bare essentials here I'm afraid."

"Are you kidding? We're safe and dry and have food to eat. And wine. It's a lovely dinner." She looked at him gratefully. "Really, Jesse, thank you." She picked up a biscuit, still hot from the oven, and took a bite. Surprisingly it was quite good just by itself.

"You're welcome, Taryn." He added softly, "I'm very much enjoying spending time with you."

She gave him a sickly smile. "Even with all that crap about my marriage I just laid on you?"

"Yes, especially with that. Which was not crap. I feel honored you would talk to me about it. Relationships are difficult."

"God, I never thought they were supposed to be. From the time I was a kid I just assumed I would find the right person and settle into something comfortable that would last a lifetime. Like my grandparents. Boy was I wrong."

"One of the great laws of the universe is change."

"Now you tell me," she laughed wryly. Then in a somber tone, "Really Jesse. Why did you say I wanted someone new? I agree that I kind of wanted out, but I never said that meant I would look for someone else."

He concentrated on eating the last of his stew while he considered. He searched her eyes for a clue—was she ready to hear this? She seemed vulnerable and unsure, but open. He took a deep breath.

"Sometimes I can read the energy behind what someone is saying. People always tell you more than what their words convey. And what I'm sensing with you is that you wanted to move on but wouldn't, so your husband did it for you." *Oh God, I didn't mean to spring that on her yet.* He sucked in his breath, hoping desperately he hadn't lost her there.

She was clearly confused, her whole body in a "what *are* you talking about?" stance.

Jesse quickly continued. "Okay, before you hit me here, can I backtrack a bit? Do you believe there's more to us than just our minds and this physical body?"

She nodded slowly, wondering where this could be going. And thinking that hitting him right now might feel pretty good.

"Do you have a sense of what that might be? Like the soul? Or the unconscious?"

She shrugged. "Of course I've heard the words, kind of know a little, from yoga. But I haven't really thought about that stuff much. My family didn't go to church, and Wyatt was never interested either. What does that have to do with what you just laid on me?"

Hearing the edge in her voice made him flustered. "A lot really.

Taryn. We don't have to talk about this if it bothers you."

She leaned forward and spat the words out before thinking. "No, you're not going to stop there, mister. You need to explain why you said all that." Her eyes opened wide. *Oh, my. There's that anger, like Eric's, Jesse'd said was just fighting against something that made you uncomfortable. Trying to take power back. Wow, it's true, what he said.*

Taryn's face and voice softened. "Sorry, Jesse. Anger isn't going to get me anywhere. Please go on. I want to hear it." She settled back and tried to open up again.

Damn, she catches on quick. She actually listened to what I said about Eric yesterday.

"Okay. Here goes. I believe we all have a piece of us that is deeply connected to the universe, life, God, whatever you want to call it— something much bigger than just the little lives we have here. It's so much more aware than our minds, which can only see what happens to be put in front of us, and even then doesn't always see things clearly. It's how I see the soul. Your soul, being so connected to the 'grand design of life' so to speak, may take your life in directions that you didn't think, with your mind, you wanted to go. Can you understand what I mean?"

"Yes, I think so," she said thoughtfully.

"When you talked about the romance novels, what I heard in the energy behind the words you didn't say is that your soul wanted out of the marriage and wanted someone new in your life."

"Why though? Lots of people, happily married people, read romance novels. Doesn't mean they want out. It's just for fun. Why did you think it was different for me?" The tone in her voice registered resistance.

"Well, I didn't think it, I felt it. Like I said, it's an energy, a sense. You're a sensitive, empathic woman, so I know you've experienced what I'm talking about here. Call it a gut feeling I had, or intuition, if those words fit better for you."

"Yeah, okay. But even if that was true, and I'm not sure the part about the 'someone new' is, why would you say Wyatt did it for me? That doesn't make any sense at all." A bit of irritation had crept back into her voice.

Tread lightly here, this is all new for her ... "Actually it does, if you can look at it another way than you're used to. Pretend we're not talking about you and Wyatt for a minute. Pretend we're watching a movie. So you can see this from the outside. Can you do that?"

Where the hell is this guy taking me? "I don't know, but I'll try." She took in a deep breath, closed her eyes, and imagined a movie screen in front of her.

"Remember we're looking at a pattern here that many people play out. See this woman, in an unhappy marriage. And her husband is unhappy too, but he doesn't show it to her. Both of them are caught up in the fairy tale of happily ever after. He's starting to let that go even though she can't yet. Still, he sees the romance novels she tries to hide in her night stand, and she's not responding to him anymore, at least not how she used to. Now he's probably not the type to do deep thinking, so all this awareness is happening mostly at an unconscious level. He's picking up on this energy she has, of wanting to get out, find someone new. But she's not leaving. The energy, the tension, keeps building and building. It shows up for him as this undefined restlessness. And eventually *he* acts it out, finds a new love. Even though it's not something he ever thought he'd do."

He watched her face carefully as he spoke, looking for signs he might have gone too far. But she was holding her own. Her mouth was set in a firm line as she concentrated on the scene in her mind.

"Can you feel what I'm talking about Taryn?" he asked with a hesitant voice that reflected his concern.

She opened her eyes, shook her head. "Not really, Jesse. I can get the unhappiness they have, and their desire to leave. And even that maybe she wanted someone new. But why would *he* cheat instead of her?"

Her shoulders tensed and brow furrowed as she struggled to understand. And she wondered why she was even subjecting herself to talking about this part of her life she so wanted to leave behind. Still, she could feel that what Jesse was saying to her was leading her to something important, something she needed to hear.

"Okay, let me add more to this scenario. Her soul wants out but she can't bring herself to do anything. She's still hung up on the dream, still not letting herself see how toxic the deadness of the marriage is for her. Her soul has all this yearning and it only has this tiny outlet to express— the romance novels. People in a marriage are strongly entwined. The energy she has spills over onto him, takes him over, even though it didn't originate with him. And he acts on it because she wouldn't."

Her frustration level hit ten as she crossed her arms and scowled at him.

Oh God, she's hit overload. Shit. Nowhere to go from here. Shit. Shit. He panicked, sat stock still, waiting for her to make the next move.

Abruptly she stood, careful to keep her quilt tightly wrapped around herself, and in a shaky voice pleaded, "Jesse, I think I just need some sleep now. Is it okay if I just go to bed?"

He cringed, and softened. "Of course, Taryn. Please remember—I'm not trying to pretend I have all the answers. I just had a gut feeling and was following a thread. I'm so sorry if all that was more than you wanted to hear ..." His eyes were filled with compassion and concern.

"No, don't apologize. I can tell you're trying to be helpful. It's just ..."

He rose and touched her briefly on the arm. "Go to bed. I'll take care of everything out here."

"Thank you. Good night, Jesse." Her voice was tight but controlled.

"Sleep well, Taryn."

Chapter

8

Yeah, like I'm going to get any sleep after that, she thought as she waddled in her quilts to her bed.

Jesse's words had turned her world upside down, and suddenly she remembered the feeling she'd had before she came to the ranch that something profound would happen here.

My God, I was right. Even more than I knew. Please can I have a do-over?

The question was barely out and already she knew she didn't mean it. However uncomfortable the conversation had made her, probably the most uncomfortable she'd ever been barring the revelation from Wyatt about his affair, she knew she'd needed to hear every word. Now. Something in her knew this night, like the night Wyatt left, was a turning point in her life.

She pulled the covers tight around her and curled up in a ball. Jesse had begun cleaning in the kitchen, and she listened to the familiar sounds of water running and dishes being stacked. They calmed her nerves enough that she could think again.

She remembered nights of lying beside Wyatt, wondering if she even knew the man anymore. So many times not a word would pass between them; good night kisses were cursory, if they happened at all. When she woke in the morning, he would already be gone. Sometimes she just lay alone for a while, feelings of despair washing over her. Then she would force herself to get out of bed and put on the face the world expected a woman in a perfect marriage to have. Sometimes she was even able to convince herself that's what she had. Mostly though she'd had to keep very busy to avoid what she now saw was the obvious truth. *Why did I do that to myself? My God, all that pretense. Was that just to please everyone else? Or was I just too embarrassed to admit I'd made a mistake? No, that's not the right word—Wyatt wasn't a mistake. We had a lot of good years. More like that I'd failed, not lived up to the dream.*

And Greta. Good grief, it was so blatant sometimes—their flirting. The way she always seemed to wind up next to him, reached out to touch his arm if he said something funny, looked at him way more than she did anyone else. Jeez, at that arts gala I watched him push the hair off her face and slowly run his fingers down her cheek. I totally saw all that. Why the hell didn't I let it register? Even though I wanted to scream at the time.

She remembered picking up that first romance novel, on a whim. She'd devoured it in a day. Went to the bookstore the next morning and bought ten more. She'd wondered for a time if it was possible to be addicted to books. Aside from her kids, reading them had been the times she felt most alive.

Okay, okay. I get that I wanted out. But how did Jesse get from "you read romance novels" to "you wanted someone else?"

A scene from her favorite novel flashed before her and the sudden rush of heat in her belly told her how. With reluctance, she admitted to herself that when she'd read it she had really—*really*—wished it could happen to her. She had so longed to be touched again, be made love to again, by a man who truly wanted her. As Wyatt had not, not for years. Images of her favorite characters marched one by one through her mind. Oh God, she wanted them. She did. She wanted to feel alive again, feel sexual again.

Desire coursed through her in waves. A noise from the kitchen brought Jesse to mind, and for a moment the image of him on stage with the band came back—tight body dressed all in black, deep sexy voice singing about love, fingers so gently controlled on the strings. For a few minutes, she indulged in fantasies of those fingers touching her, his lips roaming over her body, making love with him in all the ways she'd read about in the books.

Finally her head broke in, reminding her that the subject of her fantasies—Jesse—was in fact someone she barely knew, someone who surely didn't want her, someone definitely out of reach. Slowly the fire went out, resignation and dismay setting in again.

Okay, I get that I wanted someone else. Can't avoid that one anymore. But that bit about the energy spilling over from me to Wyatt. I really don't get that. Why would he do something just because I wanted to do it? Wyatt wouldn't do anything unless he himself wanted to. It just doesn't make sense ...

Her head spun in circles, until exhaustion finally took her over. She slept fitfully.

After Taryn went to bed, Jesse sat back down on the couch. He stared at the fire.

God, I hadn't intended for that to get so heavy. I'm not at all sure she was ready to hear it. Those perspectives are a lot to hit someone with, if they haven't done much spiritual work. Which she hasn't. For heaven's sake, even I almost left that first conference when it became clear what my nightmare about Veronica really meant. It took me the whole rest of the week to come to terms with it because it was such a blow to my ego.

And what if I'm wrong? Intuition isn't exactly foolproof.

But what I said did seem to resonate for her. There were times when I could feel her actually opening up to it all. And I still believe that first hit I had about her when our eyes met in the lodge—she's got a depth to her that's just waiting to be reached.

Oh, yeah. Pause a minute here. Remember that all you can do is offer what you see. What she does with it is up to her. If her soul isn't ready to take it in, then she won't. And she'll wake up tomorrow in the space she was in before we talked. Just hope she's not pissed off at you for getting so personal.

He took a deep breath and let it go.

The fire would need wood if it was going to make it through the night. He walked outside to get more and was not happy to see it was still snowing. Already up to a foot, maybe more. He wasn't sure they would be able to leave in the morning. He hustled back inside, stoked the fire and went to the kitchen to get himself another cup of coffee.

Thoughts of the conversation with Taryn kept coming. He knew second-guessing was futile, but it was hard not to wonder if he'd said things in such a way that she could really hear it. *God I hope she did. I just feel like this is a key that will help her get past her divorce, help her move on with her life. Oh ... Pause again. You're letting yourself get attached to the outcome. You can't do that if you really want to be of service. It's up to her soul to determine where this goes; what you might want is irrelevant here. Let it go.* He pushed the thoughts away as best he could, tried to concentrate on the cleaning tasks at hand.

But her face stayed in his mind. Big blue soulful eyes, delicate nose and soft full lips that made the sweetest smiles. Her blond hair falling in soft waves down her shoulders. As his mental picture of her moved down her body—her full breasts and hips, shapely legs—and his body lit up in response, he could not deny how much he really wanted this woman. Feelings he had pushed away for so many years came flooding back.

There had been plenty of opportunities to be with a woman since his divorce. God knows half the single women who came to the ranch had at least flirted with him. And more than a few of the married ones as well. Some had even flat-out propositioned him. His determination not to let anyone in again, not to trust again, had held them all off.

Taryn was different. She'd made no moves, in all honesty hadn't even seemed that interested in him. Maybe that was why he was so drawn to her. Well, one reason.

Jesse washed the coffee cups and pot and crawled into bed. Still in conflict with his feelings about Taryn—wanting to be close, but so unsure of himself—he tossed and turned for a while. When sleep finally overcame him, even dreams did not intrude.

Something jarred Jesse awake. He glanced at the clock. 2:45 in the morning. Gradually his ears picked up on the quiet sobs coming from the living area. He climbed out of bed and wrapped a quilt around himself. As he approached her from behind, he intentionally made enough noise to let Taryn know he was there so as not to startle her. Then he put his hand on her shoulder and sat next to her on the couch.

"Taryn. Are you okay?" he asked softly.

She lifted her tear-stained face to him, but couldn't look him in the eye yet. "I don't know Jesse. I just keep thinking of all the years I wasted, hanging on to something that needed to end. I've been such a coward."

With that, she began crying again, and Jesse instinctively reached out to hold her. He was surprised when she burrowed into him, holding on tightly. His hand stroked her hair—*oh she smells so good*—as he murmured reassurances. She moved her hand to his chest and he felt the quickening as his heart pounded. *No, no, you can't take advantage of her now.*

But she'd raised her head, her lips so very close to his, and clearly wanted to be kissed. And he couldn't resist, didn't want to. His mouth met hers, tenderly at first, then with more and more passion as they both caught fire. He pushed their quilts aside, running his hands down her back, then up her stomach to her breasts. She moaned, buried her fingers in his chest hair, moving them slowly down to his stomach.

A thought that she might not really want this, that even he might not really want this, flitted through his mind, but his desire for her was too strong now. He laid her down gently and pressed on top of her. "Jesse," she panted and pulled him to her tight. He could feel how much, how very much, she needed him, needed all of him. Her fingers caressed him, learning, yearning. She felt him shiver at her touch and her heart soared, that she could affect him so.

Caught up in the melody that was Taryn, he played her body like his guitar, his fingers shifting from chord to chord as the pressure and tempo increased. When she spread her legs wider, he slowly pushed his way inside, and she gasped with the intensity of the sensation.

He was in awe how perfect this felt, how right, to be with her. She was so in sync with his every move; their lover's dance the sweetest union. They hit the peak together, crying out in unison.

They lay panting for a minute, stunned by their love-making. Slowly he started to pull out, but she held on tight.

"Please don't," she pleaded. "Jesse ..." She was so full of need—for this sensitive man, for this experience of being wanted, for this exquisite closeness. In this suspended moment in time, she was all *feeling*.

Gently he stroked her hair, kissed her forehead. "Taryn," he whispered. "Are you all right?"

He could feel her trembling, but she nodded so he just held her. As he shifted his weight, he slid further into her and she pulled him to her greedily. Slowly he began to rock them again in an erotic rhythm. Consumed by passion, they gave up all control and let their bodies take them to the heights again.

Exhausted, they lay in silence for a while.

"Jesse, I ..." Her voice was a mixture of embarrassment and longing. "I'm so sorry."

"Shhh," he interrupted. "Don't even go there. I've wanted you from the minute I first saw you, if I'm honest with myself. It's I who should be apologizing to you, if I took advantage of you in a moment of weakness, after all we talked about."

"No. I've wanted you too, but I was afraid to show you that. You must get so sick of women throwing themselves at you. I didn't want to be one of them."

"You're not, Taryn. I can feel your sincerity. I think we both know that what just happened between us was not just casual sex; we made love." He hesitated, then drew in a deep breath. "I haven't let myself go there for a very long time."

"Neither have I," she whispered.

Again they lay in silence, each savoring the feelings and sensations of being so close. She felt safe and cared for in his warm embracing arms. He felt the gentleness of her hand on his chest, the softness of her cheek as it brushed against his. She marveled at the firmness of his thigh pressed up to hers, the depth of his brown eyes. And as he felt her tender vulnerability, her open yielding to his hands, his heart melted. *Oh God, am I falling for her? I can't do that; I know what happens when I let someone in. Oh no ...*

"Taryn, maybe we should go back to bed, get some more sleep?"

Tears sprang to her eyes as insecurity took her over. *No, no, no, is it really over already? We're going back to our separate beds? I know this wasn't a forever thing, but this is too wrenching, to be done so soon.*

Gently, he said, "Do you want us to go to your bed or mine?" He ran his fingers down her face and lifted her chin. The soft lingering kiss left no doubt—he was not done with her yet.

He pulled her with him as he got to his feet and they stood body to body, neither wanting to break apart to take the first steps. Finally he wrapped a quilt around them both and together they made it to his bed. Quickly they got under the covers and held each other close. Again their passions overcame them and they made love, hard and fast, rising and falling with an intensity like neither had felt before.

As they drifted off to sleep, he breathed, "Taryn, you're amazing."

Chapter

9

The sunlight streaming across her face finally woke Taryn in the morning. Slowly her awareness brought back the reality of the cabin, and she realized Jesse was already up and dressed. She was alone in the bed they had shared so intimately during the night. The empty space was jarring. She so wanted to reach out and snuggle up against him, feel him close. *Isn't that what people who'd connected so deeply would do? Get up and pee, sure, but then come back to bed again. Why would he just ... leave?*

I guess last night really must have been a fluke. I mean, seriously. He has his pick of most of the women who come to the ranch. Why would he be interested in me—I'm such a mess. Jeez, after all I told him about my life ... Even I'd want to run from someone as screwed up as me. Her heart sank. *Maybe that really was just a pity fuck, in spite of all those sweet things he said.* Her eyes filled with tears and she was glad he wasn't there to see them. She struggled to control her tumultuous feelings. *Nothing to do but go on as if it didn't happen then. Play it safe.*

She pulled the quilt around her and made her way to the bathroom without speaking to him. Quickly pulling on her clothes and rinsing out her mouth, she tried to put on a calm face.

Then she opened the door and, with a voice as devoid of emotion as she could get it, said, "Good morning."

The lack of any warmth in her voice threw him. Suddenly he wasn't sure where he stood with this woman. Or even where he wanted to. He managed to return the "Good morning" but couldn't think of what else to say. So he turned to the tasks at hand, poured her a cup of coffee and offered it to her silently.

She took the cup from his hand but, feeling his awkwardness, dared not look him in the face. *Oh, God. I was right. He's not even talking to me now. What happened between us last night is really gone. Oh, God. Don't let him see that you're hurt. Keep it cool. Keep it light.*

"What's it look like outside?" she asked, walking to the window and looking out. Brilliant white snow covered everything, the huge boulders and tall trees sparkling in the sun. For a moment she was mesmerized by the scene. Then she realized its implications. "Oh. Really bad, isn't it? How deep is it?"

He reluctantly followed her cue of keeping it casual. "I'd say well over two feet. It's stopped coming down now, thank goodness, but it's really too deep for the horses at this point. Even two feet wears them out pretty quickly, especially if there are drifts to go through. I think we're stuck here for another day, till it can melt some."

"Oh ..." she trailed off.

The dejected tone in her voice rattled him. Almost in a panic he blurted, "I'd better go check on the horses; then I'll make some breakfast."

She couldn't look him in the face, hearing the strong desire to bolt in his voice. She just got an "okay" out as he turned and walked through the door.

Shattered, she fell onto the couch in a heap. Hot tears burned a trail down her cheeks, and try as she might, she couldn't stop them. Her emotions were in turmoil. From Jesse's pronounced distance this morning, after such a close and tender night, to her new-found realizations about the hows and whys of Wyatt's cheating, and now the prospect of another long day with a man who didn't want to be with her—she felt there was nothing solid below her to stand on. Frantically, she looked inside for a "this end up" sign but found nothing. Huge sobs wracked her body and she tried desperately to keep them quiet at least. She hoped against hope that Jesse would stay out long enough for her to get control of herself again.

❦

Jesse slipped into automatic pilot as he fed and watered the horses, who seemed to have made it through the night just fine in their warm blankets. His focus was all on Taryn.

Good God, talk about a 180. How could we have been so ... intimate, and then flip to this crazy distance? It's madness. I get up to make coffee and she goes cold. What's with that anyway?

Damn, maybe she decided everything that happened yesterday was a mistake. Maybe I pushed her too far when we talked. God I hope she didn't think I was trying to psychoanalyze her or something. As if I could—I don't have any training for that. I told her I was just feeling into her patterns and following a thread. Like in the conferences. Trying to be helpful. What if she didn't hear it that way?

Maybe the sex was just a moment of weakness and she didn't really want that. Oh shit. Did I take advantage of her? Oh shit.

But it didn't feel that way. I mean she's the one who started it. She wanted it as much as I did. One word from her and I would have stopped.

He shook his head in frustration.

What the hell, dude—you don't even want to get involved with her. You've managed to keep women out for all these years, and you know why. Why did you let her in, even for one night? What the hell were you even thinking?

He patted the horses one last time and gathered more firewood. Then he shut his eyes tight and withdrew into himself, as he had for so long. As he walked to the cabin door, he steeled himself for what might come next.

❧

She was nearly back together—well, as together as someone can be who is splattered all over the ground in broken pieces—when Jesse opened the door and walked in with more firewood in his arms. Her swollen eyes and look of hopelessness jolted him out of the self-centered fear he'd fallen into. His heart opened wide with concern and compassion for her.

He dropped the wood and rushed to sit by her. His gentle fingers brushed the hair from her face as his lips found hers in a reassuring kiss. Then he held her close as he whispered in her ear.

"Taryn. Oh, Taryn."

Grief, man, look at it from her side. She wakes up and I'm gone, and not even friendly when I say good morning. She must have thought I don't care. She doesn't know how scared I am. How terrified I am to trust anyone again, let anyone in again. She so didn't deserve my coldness.

She didn't know what to do. She wanted to respond, to the Jesse before her now, the same one she'd felt last night. But why had he been so aloof earlier, why had he run? What if he did that again? She didn't dare open herself up to him. So she sat stiffly, waiting to see what he would do next.

He felt her reluctance, understood it. Slowly he pulled back, and looked deeply into her eyes. She was afraid to meet his gaze at first, but he held it steadily, letting her know he was not going anywhere. Finally she relented, allowed him in.

"Taryn we need to talk. I need to tell you something, about me. But I think we should have some breakfast first."

"I'm not really hungry Jesse," she said in a subdued tone that revealed her fragility. He was going to have to be more careful with her, he realized now. His distance earlier had done some real damage to whatever was happening between them.

"I can imagine," he said gently. "Still, we have a long day ahead of us, including some snow shoveling, and we need food. Please? I'll make us some pancakes ..." His eyes pleaded with her as he raised her hand to his lips, then rose from the couch.

Pancakes, she mused. That would take some time, be a very neutral thing to do, keep them busy, no emotion. Give her a chance to get herself square again. She got up and moved to the kitchen.

"What can I do to help?"

After they'd eaten and cleaned up, Jesse sent a text to Dustin.

Still doing good here. But nearly 3 feet of snow so won't be leaving soon.

Dustin's reply came quickly.

They're saying it will warm up today, lots of melting. Hang in there.

OK

BTW tell Taryn Derek's fine. Broken leg but the surgery went well.

That's good news. I'll tell her.

Jesse looked up to see Taryn's face forming a sickly smile under eyes filled with confusion. He took her hand and led her to the couch, in front of the fire he'd added to before breakfast.

"What is it, Taryn?" he asked quietly.

"I need to ask you more about what you said to me last night. I don't understand how someone's energy can spill over onto someone else. If, and I still mean if, I wanted to leave Wyatt and find a new man, how could that suddenly become something he would do?"

He'd wondered if she would bring this up again. And he knew if she did that he would have to open up his life to her in order to explain what she needed to know. He drew in his breath nervously. *Can I really tell her about this? I've never told anyone before, and I barely know her. Yeah and ... I bet she was thinking the same thing about you when she told you about reading those novels. You'd be dissing her big time if you backed out now.* As he breathed out, he let himself feel the rightness of this moment.

"Taryn, I need to tell you about a ... happening in my life."

Her eyes widened. This was new—Jesse opening up. She pulled her legs up onto the couch to sit cross-legged, facing him. "I'm listening."

"I'm sure you already know I was married once too. Veronica. Spitfire of a little lady who was the privileged daughter of a partner in the law firm I worked for. One night we got into a wicked fight, a really wicked fight, and in the heat of it all she slapped me hard across the face. Suddenly I found myself crying like a baby. Not because she'd hit me, but because in the flash of an instant I *absolutely knew* that the only reason she *could* hit me was because I *let* her. I felt it, deep, deep down, that something in me had given her permission to slap me."

The skeptical look on Taryn's face made him pause. "Look. This is really hard to explain—words can't begin to do it justice because it comes from a space that's well beyond words. And beyond any kind of blame—on her or on me. Because in that deep realm, there is no judgment. I'm not talking about giving her permission at what we would consider our normal everyday level, not saying that in my mind I agreed to this. It did not come from what we'd call ordinary consciousness, not something I thought. No way would my mind agree to that, to be hit like that, by anyone. It happened too fast for thought—like a billionth of a nanosecond. But I could *feel* that something deep in me had an agreement with something deep in her that I would let her hit me, that she could treat me like that. It was an instantaneous and complete knowing, not to be denied. A truth so pure even my mind couldn't fight it."

He dropped his head then, overcome with the emotion of remembering that slap.

Taryn scrunched up her face. "I don't understand. Why would you agree to something like that?"

"I can't really answer that, like you would want. Because the part of me that agreed was soulic, and my mind knows only a small part of my soul's true intent. And understands even less. For me, I think it was so I could learn something. So I could see the dynamic of the agreement my head hadn't known anything about. So I could see that there was a piece of me willing to subjugate myself to her."

He looked so uncomfortable, telling her all this, that she didn't know what to do. Tentatively she reached for his hand. Gratefully he responded to her touch and recovered.

"But I need to tell you the rest of the story. She left an ugly bruise on my cheek and I called in sick to work for several days. Mostly because I was in shock. All of this happened before I'd done any of the spiritual conferences I've done, back when I considered myself an atheist with a focus all on what we think of as reality, so I had nothing to guide me, no way to make any sense of it. About a week later, we had another really bad fight and at one point I could feel that energy rising in her—she was going to hit me again. Then I felt something rise up in me and say, without spoken words but with the full power of my being, '*do not even think about it.*' She backed down. And she never tried to hit me again."

His shoulders slumped, his energy spent. As he bowed his head, she marveled at his willingness to tell her about what was obviously a very private and painful experience. Then the significance of his words hit her.

"Wow, Jesse. So what are you saying? That everyone who lets someone else hit them *agrees* to it?"

"Taryn, I am only trying to speak for myself here. I can only tell you about the truth of my own experience, for me. What I'm trying to get at is that I believe people's souls make connections and agreements our minds are not aware of. My teacher finally gave me the words I didn't have back then. We make secret contracts with others in our lives. Contracts our minds aren't part of and don't comprehend. They're made at a different level—an unconscious level—of our being. And once you can really see this, you can understand that you're not a victim in the situation, but a willing participant. However uncomfortable the situation might have been, you were not as power-less as it seemed, and you can realize you have the power to deal with it. This is what I think happened with you and Wyatt."

The look of shock on her face made him grimace.

"Wyatt never hit me. Never."

"No, I didn't mean that. Secret contracts can be about all kinds of things. Most of our lives are really lived unconsciously, you know. We like to think we're in control, that we decide in our minds what we'll do, how our lives will go. But our minds are the tip of the iceberg."

"I don't get what you mean, Jesse." She furrowed her brow, puzzled by the turn of the conversation.

"Well, here's an example. What's your favorite color?"

"Uh, green I guess," she said, her consternation growing.

"Why? Do you really know? I would bet that you could come up with all sorts of reasons—it's the color of nature, it's peaceful, and so on. But I would also bet that something in you was drawn to that color even before you 'knew' why, that the reasons you have came *after* your actual choice. That something much deeper in you made that choice. Can you feel that?"

Taryn pondered this for a moment, then said, "I can. I could come up with just as many reasons to like any other color as I could to prefer green. It really wasn't my mind that chose one color over another. Is that what you're meaning about our lives being run by the unconscious?"

"Yes. And if you stay with that for a minute, you can start to see that it's not just our choices of colors that are made at that level, but pretty much every aspect of our lives. Our souls—that part of us that's the essence of who we are—works through the unconscious. Our minds are aware of only a small part of what's really going on."

It was a bit further than she wanted to go on this subject. She crossed her legs and asked pointedly, "So then what does this all have to do with Wyatt and me?"

Jesse took in a deep breath. "Sometimes secret contracts can be made when one partner agrees to take on a burden the other can't carry. Especially when someone does something out of character, it can be a sign that they've taken on doing something that their partner could not do themselves. Like Wyatt moving on to someone new because you were not able to do it yourself."

He stopped to let the words sink in.

She was very quiet, reeling from Jesse's last words. She'd accepted that the romance novels were telling her how much she wanted to leave and find someone new. And she felt into the tension that had moved unspoken in the last few years of her marriage. She could feel how the energies had built and built, crying out for release. Yet she'd done nothing. *He cheated on me to get us out of the marriage because I didn't have the courage to do it myself? Oh God.* The tears slowly fell down her cheeks as she felt the truth of this permeate every cell of her being. It was—what were Jesse's words?—an instantaneous knowing, so huge it left no room for doubt. The intensity of the pain in her eyes cut him to the core and tears sprang to his eyes as well. They sat gazing at each other intently, seeing deeply soul to soul.

Mournfully, she said, "How can I hate him now, Jesse? If I made him do that?"

"Taryn, be careful here. You can't simplify this into thinking that you made him do anything. If that's how this all went down—you being unable to make a move yourself so he did—then it was at a soulic level, not you being 'chicken' or something. It wasn't a character flaw, which is how it sounds when you say such things. To begin with, you don't really know why your soul chose not to be the one to leave the marriage. Your head thinks it's because you didn't want to give up on the fairy tale and so on, but from what I've seen in people working through relationships, reasons go far deeper than that."

"Like how? What other reason could there be?" She felt so bad, still, thinking she had somehow forced Wyatt to do something so out of character for him, something he maybe didn't even want to do. She was hoping against hope that Jesse might absolve her from that sin.

He reflected. "Well ... I'm just going to make this up here, because I certainly don't have all the answers. I can see glimpses of your soul, but of course I've not even met Wyatt. And remember, I'm just offering what my intuition is telling me. You have to decide for yourself whether it feels like it fits, for you. That said ... What if both of you knew the relationship needed to end? Again I'm talking at a deep level—at conferences we call it the soulic level—not the everyday level of consciousness. But you had this need to be a 'good girl,' not hurt him, not be the one to 'give up on love.' And his soul had a need to be rejuvenated by a woman who could see him with fresh and adoring eyes. At a soulic level you loved each other so much that you made an agreement. He would be the fall guy, the one to cause the breakup, so that your 'good person' image would remain intact. And you agreed to give him the chance to find a new relationship that would recharge him, give him a new spark. All of this is happening at an unconscious level, of course. Wyatt would *think* he was horrible to be cheating on you but would still be driven to do it even if his head couldn't figure out why. You would be hurt but not vindictive, not stand in his way."

He stopped short. She was staring at him wide-eyed and he couldn't tell if that was horror or realization on her face. It took some time before she could speak.

"Holy shit, Jesse. I can actually feel what you're saying now. I don't know if you got the agreement exactly right, but I can feel the love that went into how we ended. Under all the pain, and anger, and confusion, I can feel the love we had for each other. How can that be when things seemed so awful?"

Jesse leaned forward and held her hand.

"It's all in the way you look at it, Taryn. Simple words but so difficult to really get. If you only see the pain in the situation, and ignore the fact that change was necessary and that it would be uncomfortable, then you're left with nothing but the pain. All you can feel is how hurt you were that he cheated on you and left. But when you see it all through the lens of that second part—the necessity and the discomfort of change—you see its value and its purpose. You can see that you both needed to move on, and that it wouldn't be easy to get yourselves separated. And now you can begin to see the love driving it."

He could tell she'd gone away, into the past. He waited for her to come back.

"I remember that day when we were at the lawyer's office, going through the details of our separation agreement. I'd just walked out of the room to get some water, and I heard Wyatt tell his attorney 'give her whatever she wants.' It shook me—that he would be so generous, and I could hear the caring in his tone when he said it. At the time I just thought he was saying that out of guilt, but now, after what you've said ... He really did care."

"I'm sure he did Taryn," Jesse said softly.

"And I know I still did too. Somehow, even though we were breaking things up, we were still in sync, still working toward the same goal." Her voice was filled with wonder.

"Yes, you see what I mean. At some deep level both of you understood what needed to happen and moved through it together." He smiled, in awe once again of how the simple act of seeing things from a different perspective could turn a life.

"It's amazing. I know you said to not just take your word for all this, take just what really felt right to me. Well, this feels exactly right. I feel like a ten-ton weight has just been lifted from me. Like the pain and anger and confusion don't even matter anymore. Jesse ..."

The tears were flowing again, but this time they were tears of relief. He gently stroked her cheek, his own eyes filled with admiration for this brave woman. He so wanted to take her in his arms, make love to her but he knew he could not intrude in this delicate space she was in.

"I'm so happy for you. And, I know from my work in conferences that when someone has reached the point you've reached, it is very important to give them time alone to let the realizations settle in. Can you feel that what I'm saying is true?"

She nodded, grateful that he understood.

"So I'm going to let you have the cabin to yourself for a little bit, while I do some shoveling and tend to the horses. Are you okay with that?"

Again she nodded. Then she leaned forward and kissed him tenderly. It took every ounce of his control to let his lips leave hers, then stand. He gave her his warmest smile, then turned and quietly walked out the door.

Chapter

10

Taryn sat in stunned silence for many minutes and let the feelings wash over her. There were no words, no thoughts, but she could feel the swirlings inside her, the movement of deep level change. Things shifted. And released. And fell into place. She breathed more deeply, more fully. She knew she would never be the same again.

Finally the transformations bubbled up from the deeper level to her normal awareness; the words came in waves.

My God, it's true. The whole process was done in love. Even though he left for another woman, Wyatt never treated me with anything other than respect, never put me down or said mean things to me, always made sure I was taken care of. I remember that so many of our friends told me how nicely the divorce was going compared to others they'd seen, some of them even asking why I wasn't more upset. And he's continued to be that way—with me, with the kids. I couldn't see it before because I could only see the pain, but that was his love showing through.

She thought back to the night he'd come home to tell her about his affair with Greta. Looking at it all through new eyes, she could see how truly horrified he was to have to say those words to her, could see in his posture that some part of him actually wanted to reach out to console her. The caring for her had not died, even if it was no longer the kind of love he'd once felt for her and had now given to another.

Wow, and if I look at how I was with him ... Even though I felt so angry and hurt, I never went for revenge or got vindictive. I made sure the settlement agreement was fair to him too, never tried to turn the kids against him. Because of the love I had for him. Had? Have, still. It's different now, but it really is still there—the love and respect. Wow. Wow.

And Jesse's right. If Wyatt and I agreed to have us end that way then I really wasn't some kind of victim. I was part of it all along. Yeah it was embarrassing that he cheated on me, that it took so long for me to realize it, that he left me for her. It hurt a lot. But it got me free of a marriage that was, actually, killing me, killing both of us. Now we can live our lives. Oh my God, what an amazing journey we've been on.

She could hear Jesse outside; he was shoveling. She rose and peeked out the window. The snow was seriously melting now, the sun shining brightly, thank goodness. She watched him work, this wonderful man who had opened her heart and her awareness in such a miraculous way. An overwhelming gratitude filled her and even though he would never see, she bowed her head to him.

The simple act of moving her head suddenly brought her body into focus and she realized two things—she desperately needed to pee, and she was hungry. Quickly she took care of the first need, then went to the door to ask Jesse about lunch.

She was about to call out to him when abruptly he stopped shoveling and just stood looking at the beauty of the mountains. The sight of him, strong and compassionate and so appreciative of the scene before him, sent shivers of awe and desire through her. Not for a very long time had she felt so alive. She waited until he moved again, then spoke.

"Jesse, I was thinking about making some lunch. You up for that?"

He turned and gave her a dazzling smile.

"Oh, yes, Taryn. That would be great. I'll be right in."

Jesse took a quick sponge bath while Taryn scouted in the kitchen for something to make for lunch. Options were limited, of course, since there was no electricity. Only foods that could be cooked on the propane stove or propane oven or required no cooking at all were available. Still, she spotted a can of spiced chicken, a can of mushroom soup and some wide noodles. Add a bit of the white wine left over from the night before and *violá*—a nice pasta dish. She found a large pot and filled it with water, lit the stove and got it boiling. She was about to put the noodles in when Jesse walked into the room.

"Okay I feel better. Probably smell a bit better too," he said as he raised his arm and pretended to sniff.

"I'm making us some pasta. That work for you?"

"Yeah, that sounds good. I'll see if there's another bottle of wine to go with."

"Oh yes, please," she agreed as he moved to the cabinet at the end of the counter and retrieved a bottle of Merlot.

Jesse turned around just in time to see Taryn standing on tip toe, trying to reach the can of chicken on the top shelf.

"Here, let me help you," he said as he moved to her side and wrapped his fingers around the can. Suddenly both were aware of their bodies touching, his chest against her breast, her hip lightly brushing his crotch, their heads just a breath away.

His breath caught in his throat. Heart pounding, he just managed to get the can to the counter before he wrapped both arms around her and kissed her passionately.

"Taryn," he whispered huskily.

She responded hungrily, with a smoldering kiss that sent a rush of heat through his body.

"Oh, Jesse. Please. Take me. Now," she cried, her eyes dark with want.

With one strong swift motion he had her sitting before him on the counter. He looked briefly into her eyes, saw the longing there, felt his own longing. They made love urgently, both of them wound so tightly, and the release they craved reached its full intensity then crashed over them in pulsating waves.

Jesse's deep moan echoed her own feelings of delicious satisfaction.

"God, what you do to me, woman," he breathed.

"You too, mister." Suddenly she felt shy and looked away. "Jesse, I've never felt like this with anyone before ..."

Jesse gently lifted her chin, gazed directly into her eyes.

"Taryn, you're very special."

He kissed her softly, then with a twinkle in his eye said, "Want to do lunch naked? I really like you like this."

She blushed but replied, "I kind of like you this way too." She looked him over, head to toe, then fixing her eyes below his waist, "Yes, very nice view indeed."

He laughed, and scooping her off the counter, twirled her around.

"Come on, let's finish that pasta."

They had fun making lunch, frequently interrupting the tasks at hand with groping and caressing and kissing. By the time the meal was ready though, Taryn was getting a bit chilled without clothes, so they reluctantly got dressed.

Jesse had made another fire, mostly for the warmth, and they sat down in front of it to eat. They were quiet for a while, enjoying the cozy ambiance. Taryn broke the silence.

"Jesse, would you tell me more about what happens at these spiritual conferences you went to? I have no idea what those could be like."

"Sure." He paused, to decide how to begin. "As you can guess, they were intended to get you out of your normal mindset, expand your views of life. Which means first that you really had to get out of your normal routine, be away from work and people you usually interact with. No TV, news, phones. Kind of like going into a bubble where you could get in touch with *you*, the deepest parts of you. So the conference center I went to was fairly remote, in the middle of Ohio. Most of the conferences lasted ten days, so we could all get fully immersed in the energies."

"Ten? How could you be away from your life for that long?"

"It's not as hard as you'd think. In fact, after a few days it's quite blissful to be so detached from whatever craziness your life has been to that point." He closed his eyes, feeling again the peace of the experience. "The conference itself was meditation, lots of time to yourself to deepen into what you're learning, even several days of complete silence. And the sessions with the teacher. They were about working with dreams, talking about issues or problems in people's lives. From a more expansive perspective than you normally would see things. Going way below the surface to see patterns, see the overarching themes in your life. Which help you understand who you really are, and why you do what you do." He stopped short. "Sorry. That was probably more than you wanted to know."

"No, that helps actually. I think I get a sense of what the conferences were, and why they had such an impact on you. Do you still go to them?"

"No. The teacher passed away, six years ago now," he answered quietly. "I was lucky to have had the time with him that I did have."

"I'm sorry, Jesse. Sounds like that was an important part of your life." Wistfully, she added, "I wish I could have gone to some of those conferences, especially right after ..."

"I do too, Taryn. I think you would have gotten a lot out of them." Jesse smiled at her.

Taryn squirmed, then straightened and faced him squarely. "Okay, enough about me for a while. Tell me what happened with your marriage, your divorce."

He glanced at her warily, saying, "You don't really want to hear about that."

She scowled. "Oh yes I do, Jesse. I spilled my guts; now it's your turn."

He looked so uncomfortable, she almost wanted to take it back. But she needed to know more about this man who had opened her up, brought her alive, in ways she could never have thought possible. She cocked her head and waited.

He took in a jagged breath.

"Well as I told you before—I was an attorney at a law firm in Chicago. Veronica was one of the partner's daughter. We met at the Christmas party just after I'd started working there. She was vivacious, smart as a whip and charming beyond words. Totally devoted to her father. Unfortunately, as I found out later."

Taryn's puzzled expression made him pause.

"Turned out she was more devoted to her father than to me, to us." He sighed. "Remember the wicked fight I told you about? The firm was doing this massive real estate deal and even though I was only an associate, I had access to all the relevant documents. While I was researching some background files, I ran across a company that was involved and the list of directors of that company included Veronica's father. It was a serious conflict of interest which had not been disclosed to the client. That's a really bad thing, in case you didn't know."

"Yeah, I know that much from watching movies."

"I went home that night and told Veronica about it. Know what she said? She told me to keep my mouth shut. She said not to rat out her dad. She said it wouldn't matter anyway. And it would ruin my chances of ever becoming a partner in the firm if I talked."

He looked away and his mouth set in a firm line as he thought back to that night.

"I tried to talk sense into her. Told her the law on point, explained the ramifications if someone else found out later. She wouldn't budge. Finally I lost my cool and said I'd just quit the firm, find some other firm to work at. That's when she hit me."

His eyes flared, then calmed as he went through the experience again. She waited patiently, knowing he needed to get it all out.

"You already know about that part. And that I left. That was the main reason for the divorce, knowing that I was essentially insignificant to her. Knowing where her loyalties really lay—with her father and not with me. Suddenly I realized our marriage was just a sham, a front. Frankly, it shattered my trust in women. I haven't been in a relationship since. I just can't let anyone in ..."

He hardly dared look her in the eye, but she reached out her hand and gently touched his. When at last his gaze met hers, her face showed nothing but tenderness.

"Jesse. You're so much wiser than I am. Look at all you've taught me in just the last day. Things I never would have thought of myself."

He started to protest but she put her fingers on his lips to quiet him.

"So it really surprises me that you let that one incident completely—what did you say? shatter—your trust in women. All women, just because of what one of them did? And it makes me wonder what you mean when you say the word trust."

"What are you getting at Taryn?" he asked pensively.

"Well, while we clean up the lunch dishes, can I share a story about trust, from my life?"

Jesse nodded, intrigued. They moved to the kitchen area, where Taryn continued.

"When my daughter Amy was in high school she ... uh ... holy cow I actually don't remember now what she did. But it was something she wasn't supposed to do and I went off on her. Told her I couldn't trust her anymore. Then I stopped dead in my tracks. It hit me like a ton of bricks, what I really meant when I said the word trust. What it really meant was whether I could feel confident that she would do what I expected her to do. Whether she would conform to how I thought she should behave. Like her life was supposed to be lived according to my standards, my desires. I didn't tell her what I was thinking. I still wanted her to get she'd broken a rule. But it sure got me off my high horse."

He peered at her intently. "Okay, I can kind of see that. But then what does trust mean to you now?"

"Well I guess my definition has changed into something like 'I hope your actions will be in sync with what I can accept in my life' or maybe 'can I count on you to do what you've said you'll do.'"

"But how can you be with people who don't? Like Wyatt? Didn't you say he said he'd never cheat on you? When he did, didn't that make you lose your trust in him?"

"Obviously it shook me. And I can see what you're saying, but it felt more like a 'oh he's not who I thought he was' than an 'I can't trust him at all anymore' thing. Can you get the difference? Like he gets to do what he wants with his life, and, I get to decide if his way of being matches enough with what I want for me to want him in my life."

Taryn took his hand and led him back to the couch. They sat facing each other, knees touching. Gently, she put her hand over his heart. Jesse leaned forward, concentrating hard on the meaning in her words.

"So what would you have done in my situation? She totally betrayed me, betrayed us," he asked.

"Is that so different than what Wyatt did to me, to us? God it hurt so much, and I didn't understand how he could cheat like that. But it didn't make me feel like 'I could never trust again,'" she put the back of her hand to her forehead in a mock swoon.

He couldn't help but chuckle. "Taryn, you're a treasure! But you didn't answer my question. What would you have done?"

"Assuming I could get past the pain and all, I'd have decided she just didn't share the same morals as me, she didn't value our relationship like I did, so I would be better off finding someone else. As you sort of did. Get out and find something that matches."

He thought for a minute, trying to see things from the angle she was seeing them.

"Okay, I think I get where you're coming from," he said. "Using the word 'trust' is too much a blanket statement, it throws too much onto the other person. As soon as you say 'I trust you' it dumps my expectations all over you. Which makes you just an extension of myself, not really a separate person with your own life to live. And what you're saying is to look at each situation just as it is, then ask—is this too far from what I value to want to continue to be with this person. Is that it?"

"Yes. Or maybe, like with my daughter, you see what they did was not really in sync with your values but you decide that you can live with it," she said. "My love for Amy certainly overcame the lie she told me. Especially since she was a teenager at the time—they're supposed to disobey their parents. Contrast that with what Wyatt did. Even if he had wanted to stay together after his affair, I couldn't have lived with that. Knowing that his belief about what marriage means did not match mine made it impossible for me to want to be with him anymore." She paused. "Of course in this scenario I'm conveniently leaving out the fact that he actually left me. To illustrate the point."

Her expression of heavy sadness told him how difficult it continued to be for her. He kissed her tenderly.

"Now, Jesse, in light of all that, how do you feel about trusting other women? Are we all still in the doghouse?"

He was silent for a bit, clearly wrestling with something. At last he spoke with sadness in his voice.

"I really do hear what you're saying. I do. And my head can make sense of it. But something in me is still just too afraid to take a chance again. Like it could not handle being betrayed again. Oh, God, who's the chicken now?" He dropped his head into his hands, too embarrassed to look her in the eye.

"Jesse, I don't know much about these things."

He gave her a stern look and started to speak, but she cut him off.

"Really, I don't. So think for a minute. What would your teacher have said about this?"

Again he fell silent, and closing his eyes, he pictured himself back at the conference center, surrounded by others on the path, his teacher calmly listening to him and intuiting what lay underneath his fear. Amazingly, and with great clarity, he heard what his teacher would say.

"Wow. It really comes down to control. I'm afraid she—whoever I've opened myself up to in a relationship—will do what she pleases, not what I want her to do. Which will mean I don't control her or the situation. Which means life isn't always how I want it to be. Which means the world is not revolving around me. How self-centered and childish is that?" He was incredulous.

"Yes!" Taryn said excitedly. "That's a much better way to say what I meant."

"And what my teacher said, many times to people with other issues, is that true control is about being able to react or act appropriately in a given situation, based on what's actually in front of you. It's not in making the situation be how you wanted it to be. A very subtle but distinct difference."

"Okay, so do you think maybe you could 'trust' me now?" Taryn asked expectantly. The twinkle in her eye made Jesse laugh.

"That was certainly a gottcha moment." He looked hopefully into her eyes. "I guess we'll see how deeply that realization actually went in me, how much long-term effect it will have." Softly he stroked her cheek. "I do know I'd like to trust you."

"Then do, Jesse," she said gently.

"Now, I'm going to call you out on something. You keep protesting that you 'don't know much about these things,' not as much as me or my teacher. But look what you've just taught me. I've been hiding out for years—afraid to trust again, and in a few short minutes, a few words from you, and I can start to see past it. I think you're going to have to face it—you're a wise woman."

Her eyes went wide with surprise, and she started to disagree—again—but suddenly realized she couldn't. Slowly, shyly, she smiled.

He leaned in to kiss her. He could see in her eyes she was ready again too, when his phone pinged. With a resigned shrug, he got up to retrieve it.

Hey. Jim and I are getting the snowmobiles ready. Figure we'll pack down a path for the horses to come out on. Not sure how long it will take. Melting fast down here. How's it on your end?

Jesse showed the text to Taryn, then typed a reply.

Snow has a ways to go up here. I shoveled some but it's still deep enough it would be hard on the horses.

See you in a while then.

Jesse looked longingly at Taryn. "We probably have at least an hour ..."

He trailed off as both of them realized the time in their own little bubble was about to end. With a cry, she jumped up and grabbed his hand to lead him to the bed.

Quickly they undressed each other, caressing as they went. Their lovemaking was tender and deliberate, to savor every moment. When they lay side by side, spent, they gazed into each other's eyes, seeing deeply into each other's souls.

"Taryn, you're very special. I have cherished this time with you."

She started. She couldn't tell from his tone—was he saying it was now over between them? There was such a finality to his words. She knew they were going back to the ranch, where they couldn't behave as they had in the cabin. She'd heard what Dustin told Paige about not "fraternizing" with the guests. But did it have to end completely?

All her insecurity and fears that he might not really want her came rushing back. Her shaky emotional state from all the talk and shifts and changes, even the old feelings of Wyatt's rejection, completely took her over. She was devastated.

He felt her draw back, and was about to ask her what was wrong when they heard the intrusive sounds of the snowmobiles approaching. In a panic they leaped out of bed and threw on their clothes. Quickly Taryn ran to the bathroom to try to comb out her tousled hair with her fingers while Jesse smoothed the bed covers.

Chapter

11

Jesse already had the door open as Dustin and Jim rode up. He waved hello as Taryn made an appearance at his side.

Dustin strode to the door and started to ask if they'd been okay when he saw the expressions on their faces—Jesse slightly guilty but sated, Taryn clearly a woman who'd been bedded, if a little uncomfortable at the moment. He broke out into a grin and said, "Well don't you two look fine. Should Jim and I just turn around and go back home?"

Jesse gave him a "keep it quiet in front of Jim" look and said, as calmly as he could, "Glad to see you both. And I'm sure the horses will appreciate being able to get back to their own cozy barn."

He turned to Taryn. "Would you mind making a list of everything we used while we were here? We'll need to re-stock when we can. Dustin and I will start saddling Lucky and Star."

Taryn gave him a weak smile but said, "Sure." She turned to her task.

Jesse frowned, puzzled at her distance, then also turned to his tasks.

When everything was ready to go, Taryn walked over to Dustin, who was standing by his snowmobile.

"Do you think it might be possible for me to ride back with you? Maybe Jesse can just lead Star behind Lucky? I'm not sure I'm up for a horseback ride right now."

Dustin looked at Jesse, slightly stunned. Perhaps he'd misread the situation earlier. "That okay with you, boss?" he asked.

Jesse coughed, dropped his head. He couldn't look at Taryn now, or talk openly with her. So he just said, "That would be fine."

He watched in confusion as she got on the snowmobile behind Dustin and they took off. Dismayed, he saddled the horses for the long ride home.

⁓

The snowmobiles made it back to the ranch way ahead of Jesse and the horses. As soon as they arrived, Taryn hurriedly thanked Dustin and disappeared to her cabin.

Inside, she grabbed her phone and called Paige.

"How's Derek? And how are you? God I'm sorry I've not been here for you."

"No problem, really. It was a bad break, right leg, spiral fracture. But he came through the surgery fine and should mend almost as good as new."

"I'm so relieved to hear that. How are you holding up?"

"Okay. Dustin was so sweet to me on the ride to the airport. I was actually calm when I got on the plane. He's a real gem, Taryn. I think I might be falling a little ..."

Taryn chuckled. "Do you want me to come back to Seattle to be with you? I can leave tonight." She both hoped for and feared the possibility of leaving Jesse.

"No, don't do that. Derek is insisting I go back to the ranch, finish out my prize vacation. He'll be in the hospital for a couple more days and Charlotte is watching out for him. They're so cute together by the way, and I have lots to tell you about that when I see you. So I'll be there tomorrow. But right now I gotta run."

"Oh how cool. I can't wait to see you."

"Me too, girlfriend. Bye."

It would be good to see Paige again; Taryn had so much to tell her. Jesse, and their time together. The things she'd learned about her divorce. The connection she'd made with this wise cowboy.

Jesse. She was convinced his last words—"I have cherished this time with you"—were words a man uses to end it, that it was now over between them. Just a fling in the cabin, not to be continued in their real lives. She fell on her bed in a heap, sobbing, emotions out of control. Try as she might, she couldn't figure out which end was up. Finally she cried herself to sleep.

She woke just after five. Dinner time at six. Jesse would be there. A tear rolled down her temple and pooled in her ear. She seriously considered just staying in her cabin so she wouldn't have to face him. Her heart ached.

But a little voice inside said "bawk, bawk" and she knew she had to stop being a chicken. Besides, in spite of the knots in her stomach, she was hungry. The meals in the cabin had been a bit sparse.

It took several applications of a cold washcloth over her eyes to reduce the puffiness. And a quick shower to wash off her time in the cabin. Clean clothes, fresh makeup and a practiced smile got her to the point where she felt together again. Well, enough to eat dinner with the other guests. She walked slowly to the lodge.

As soon as she sat down, everyone, of course, wanted to know all about her adventure. Jesse was nowhere to be seen, so Taryn relaxed somewhat and told the others about the snow storm, the hunters' cabin, the rescue by snowmobile. She filled in as many details as she could to make it a good story, but left out all the parts that to her had been the most important. The conversations she and Jesse had had were too sacred, too intimate to share with anyone yet. As she was finishing, Jesse came into the room to announce the plans for the evening. He carefully avoided looking at Taryn, since he now had no idea what was going on with her. *What did I do that made her pull away so hard? We were so close at the cabin, so wonderfully close. And she just disappeared ...*

"Hi everyone. I trust dinner was to your liking."

Heads nodded and compliments were given. All except Taryn who had cringed at hearing the word "trust." Jesse's use of it felt like some kind of cruel joke; she couldn't understand why he was being this way.

He continued, in as level a tone as he could muster. "Tonight is game night, for those of you who are interested. Card games, board games, even video games for all you computer types." He glanced at Eric and smiled. "They're all set out for you in the meeting room, just there." He pointed in the direction.

Taryn got up and said heavily, "I think I'll pass. I'm still tired from ... all that snow. Good night, everyone." She found she didn't have the nerve to look at Jesse, so she just left.

Dustin watched from a distance. Finally he could stand it no more. He walked to Jesse and quietly said, "Dude I don't know what happened in that cabin, but Taryn is miserable. She barely spoke to me the whole ride down, and I think she was crying. Claimed to just be shaking from the cold but ... You gotta to talk to her."

Jesse looked uncertain.

"Go, man. I got the games," Dustin insisted.

He could tell Dustin was about to physically push him out the door, so Jesse turned and followed Taryn to her cabin.

He called out to her as she reached for the door handle. "Taryn, Taryn. Please, can we talk about whatever's going on? I don't understand why you seem so unhappy."

She paused, not at all sure she wanted to hear what he might have to say. The manners her mother had drummed into her from childhood could not allow her to be rude though, so she found herself inviting him in.

They sat silently for a minute, he on the one chair in the room, she on the edge of the bed. It was Jesse who plucked up the courage to begin.

"Have I done or said something? Because if so, I honestly don't know what it is."

She dropped her head. "Your words—'I have cherished this time with you'—they sounded final, like the cabin was all there was ever going to be, like it's over now. And I get it—I'm just a guest you can't be involved with—but it felt harsh, how it ended, and I haven't got it all processed yet." Flushed, she couldn't yet look him in the eye.

Suddenly it all fell into place for him. Taryn's unsettled emotional state from what had been some rather radical shifts, the sudden ending of their time together. He'd known how fragile she was; so much had changed for her in a very short time. Of course her vulnerability would leave her shaky and uncertain, even of him.

"Taryn, no! Oh God. Is that what you thought? Do you remember that we were interrupted by the snowmobiles? There was so much more to say ..."

He crossed to the bed and reached for her, wrapped her in his arms, kissed her cheek. The sudden flip, from despair to hope, toppled what little self-control she had left, and she cried into his shoulder.

"Darling." He was stunned. He'd never used that term of endearment with anyone, ever. The word had erupted from a place he hadn't realized he'd come to yet. "I'm so very sorry to have caused you pain. You've been through a lot in the past couple of days, emotionally, with all the things we've talked about. Please tell me what I can do to help you feel safe again."

She wrapped her arms around his waist, snuggling into him. "Could you just hold me for a minute? I need to feel you with me."

"Of course, Taryn. Holding you is one of my favorite things to do." He kissed her softly on the top of her head.

Folding his arms around her gently, he lightly stroked her hair. He scolded himself for his thoughtlessness, lack of attention. He knew that people who'd had major shifts of perspective were left with a tenuous hold on their inner balance, until the shift could be assimilated, that it takes time to get re-aligned from former beliefs to new understandings. Of course she was on an emotional roller coaster. Why had he not kept a more careful eye on her, as she went through this process?

She stirred, lifted her head to face him. He put a hand under her chin and pulled her lips to his, kissing her with a tenderness she needed more desperately than she'd realized.

Slowly releasing her, he asked "Do you think you're ready to continue what was so badly cut short in the cabin?"

Not yet able to speak herself, she nodded.

"Let's see. We left off with 'I have cherished this time with you,' right? Do you remember me saying, just before that, how you're very special to me?"

Finally able to at least look him in the eye, she nodded again.

"Well next up was going to be how I don't want this to end. I don't know what 'this' is between us, have no idea where it's going, but it's too important to me, you're too important to me, to let it be just a fling in a cabin."

Before he could continue, she threw her arms around his neck and pushed him down on the bed. On top of him, pressing her body to his, her lips to his, she let it be known in no uncertain terms that she wanted him, now. His response was instantaneous as he grabbed her to him, hard.

Then coming to his senses, his hands moved to her face and he pulled his head an inch away from hers.

"God, Taryn, I want you too, so badly. But we have to finish talking first. Please?"

Had his tone not been so plaintive, she might have been afraid of what he still had to say. Reluctantly she sat up, but kept her hand suggestively on his upper thigh. He groaned.

"We have a complication here. You're a guest at a commercial dude ranch, and I'm the owner. We can't be down here as we were in the cabin. The host screwing the guests is not the image I want to present to the world, no matter how important you are to me. It would ruin me. Do you see that?" He was pleading with her, knowing that if she didn't agree to keep it cool, insisted on being open with their affections, he probably wouldn't be able to resist her.

But she sighed heavily, moved her hand to her own lap and said sadly, "I get that Jesse, I do. Surely we can work this out. I can't stand the thought of being so near you yet not allowed to touch you."

Relief mixed with angst in his voice as he replied, "Tell me about it Taryn. I don't want to hide what we are; I'm happy about us. We need to be discreet though, and I have no idea yet how we can be together," he emphasized the word, "without the others knowing. If you have ideas, by all means let me know."

"I will certainly think about it. I want this to be good for you, not a problem." She cocked her head to one side. "Didn't you say everyone else is doing games tonight? So we might have time right now?" Her hand slipped to his thigh again.

He gave her a dazzling smile. "You know, I think you're right."

They made love passionately, happily, content that though they had no clue what the future might look like, there was in fact going to be a future.

Game night was going well. Eric and Mark were battling it out on a video game, while the others played Monopoly. Ichika was winning handily, to the chagrin of Kaito. Dustin had been tending to some last minute admin details in the office and was about to leave for the night when his ears caught the drift of the conversation around the Monopoly table.

"Okay, what do you guys think really happened in that cabin between Jesse and Taryn? Something is definitely going on there." Kathy hoped this wasn't a taboo subject to bring up.

Ichika jumped right in. "I agree. It has been clear from the first night that they like each other."

"I bet there was plenty going on in that cabin," Kaito said, making a suggestive face.

Eric didn't like where this was going and broke in. "Hey, this is my girl you're talking about. I've had her in my sights since we met at the airport."

Everyone else laughed.

"Eric, get a clue. She's been trying to hold you off ever since. Taryn's eye is on Jesse." Kathy said emphatically.

Eric shrugged and turned back to his game.

"Jesse. He probably has his pick of the women who come here." Tadao said with a trace of envy in his voice.

Dustin peeked his head around the corner, anxious to nip this in the bud.

"So I don't know for sure what's going on between Jesse and Taryn, but I can tell you one thing. Jesse doesn't go after the women who come here to be ranch guests. They go after him, boy do they, but he's not the type to play around." He paused, thinking he might have been too forceful in his defense of his friend. "I just don't want you all to have the wrong idea of him."

"Got it," Kathy said sheepishly. "Sorry, Dustin. Maybe we should cool it with the gossip a bit, get back to our game. So whose turn is it?"

Chapter

12

Dustin caught Jesse the next morning as he was leaving his house.

"Hey, Jesse. Hold up," he called out. Jesse stopped and waited for Dustin to catch up.

"So, I thought you should know. Last night while everyone was playing games there was talk about you and Taryn. They all think something is going on. Actually Paige told me that too before she left."

Jesse was taken aback. "What did you say?"

"I told them I didn't know for sure. But when one of the guys said something about how you must get a lot of action from the women who come here, I did tell them in no uncertain terms that you weren't like that."

"Thanks, buddy. Man, last thing I need is to get a rep for hitting on the guests," Jesse said, his voice a mixture of relief and nervousness.

"What I didn't say is that I've never seen you so smitten. At least that's how it looks to me. Just how into this Taryn are you?"

"I wish I could answer that Dustin, but I hardly know myself." He looked wistfully in the direction of the hunters' cabin, remembering. "She certainly is something."

"That she is, boss. You'd have my blessing. And I suspect everyone else's too. Well except Eric. He'd marked her for himself."

Jesse chuckled. "No way."

"Yeah, she saw through that dud first day, at the bar." He paused. "Did I say 'dud' instead of 'dude?' Slip of the tongue."

"A good one," Jesse said mirthfully. "Thanks for telling me all this."

"Well I wanted you to get that you probably don't need to be tip-toeing around with Taryn. People have already accepted you've got something there." He smiled. "Now, to some business. Paige texted me this morning that she's coming back. Arrives on the 10:30. Mind if I go pick her up?"

Jesse playfully pushed Dustin's arm. "Now who's smitten?"

Dustin grinned sheepishly.

Jesse chuckled. "Of course you can go. Why don't you have lunch in town too, get caught up so to speak." He paused to consider. "You know I think it's pretty obvious to everyone that you and Paige have a thing going. When she gets back, you might as well be open about it. At least until the barbeque, with town folk and guests from B&Bs here. We'll both need to cool it then."

"Thanks, boss," Dustin said gratefully. "We're a pair, aren't we?"

"Indeed we are."

Taryn gave Jesse a furtive, loving glance as she walked into the dining hall for breakfast. To her immense surprise, he strode over, took her in his arms and gave her a deep kiss that clearly marked her as "his woman." When she could come up for air she gasped. "Jesse! What the..."

It was then she heard the clapping, and cheering. Turning around, she caught the delighted looks on the faces of her fellow ranch guests.

"Dustin told me everyone already knows." Jesse said with a grin. "So we don't need to hide after all." He whispered, "but we might not want to go overboard with the PDA."

Taryn blushed happily and did a quick curtsy.

She whispered, "What about the staff? Don't we need to be careful around them?"

"NDAs, all of them."

The perplexed look on her face made him smile. "Non-disclosure agreements. No one on this ranch tells secrets about anyone else, whether other staff or the guests. Especially the guests; protects their privacy. Standard stuff."

"Of course. You're an attorney," she said. "I should have known."

As Taryn took her place at the table, Jesse announced, "Paige will be returning today. Her son is doing fine. Dustin will be leaving shortly to pick her up at the airport."

"Oh, that's great news," exclaimed Kathy. "I've missed her plucky spirit around here." She looked directly at Dustin and winked.

Jesse smiled in amusement. Still, he had another announcement to make.

"One more thing everyone. We've had to change plans for the afternoon. The snow's nearly gone but it's too muddy to do any of the usual activities like paintball, the photography hike, or even a trail ride. We thought we might show a movie, make some popcorn. How does that sound to you all?"

"Like a lot of fun. What movie?" asked Kathy.

"How about *The Wife*? Have you seen it?" Jesse threw the title out with a casual tone, but he had a reason for picking that movie and hoped they would all agree.

"No, I haven't. Heard it was really good, so I'm in," Kathy said. "Didn't Glenn get nominated for an Oscar?"

"Yes I believe so," said Jesse. "Shall we say 2:00 then? Here in the lodge. We'll set up chairs in the lounge so you can be comfy."

"Sounds good to ..." Taryn started to say. Dustin interrupted by tapping her on the shoulder.

"Hey when you're done eating, how about we get with Jesse and Bobby and try calling Heather? The barbecue is tomorrow night so we don't have a lot of time left."

"Sure. Where should I meet you? Kitchen maybe?"

"That works. See you in about fifteen?"

Taryn nodded, quickly shoveling another bite of omelette into her mouth as Dustin walked away.

The kitchen was a stark contrast to the rustic lobby and dining hall; it was sleek and modern and gleaming with stainless steel. An assistant cook with a starched white apron was busy chopping vegetables and kneading bread, already well into the preparations for lunch. The woman who had spilled the wine on the first night smiled at her and quickly went back to her task of clearing the tables. Bobby had his reggae music on which made the atmosphere relaxed, even though everyone was working diligently. As she caught Bobby's eye, she gave him a thumbs up and bobbed her head to the rhythmic tune. He grinned and came out from behind the prep area to greet her.

"Eh ..."

She gave him a quick hug just as Jesse and Dustin walked in. They all crammed into Bobby's small office and called Heather at the hospital. As soon as she answered, Bobby put her on speaker.

"Hey, Heather, how are you doin'? We're so sorry to hear what happened," Jesse began.

"Oh man. It was so stupid. I just took a corner too fast and lost control, smashed into a tree. Cannot even believe I did that. Doc says I should mend well, but it will take time."

"That's great to hear. We're all thinking about you."

"Thanks, Jesse. So you have someone who can help with the barbeque?"

"Yes. Heather, meet Taryn."

"Hi, Taryn. Great to meet you."

"Hi, Heather. It's nice to meet you too, though I wish the circumstances were different."

"You and me both," Heather laughed.

Jesse continued. "So she's a guest here but has organized a lot of social events and offered to help us out. We were thinking that if you could just give her a basic idea of what needs to be done we might be able to pull this thing off."

"Sure. Well the first thing I do is contact the bed and breakfasts who will be sending their guests over. Get a head count, find out any special dietary restrictions. Bobby will handle the food from there, once he knows what's really needed. Then I pick a theme, for the decorations and such. It's usually a movie, like last time I did *Star Wars*. But since you're on a short time line here, you could keep it simple."

Taryn broke in. "Is there a budget for this, Jesse? I need to know what I have to work with. And maybe you could show me what you already have on hand."

"Yeah, we can talk more about that after we finish the call with Heather. Don't want to wear her out."

"Thanks, Jesse," said Heather. "They've got me on these drugs right now that keep me feeling a bit drowsy. Let's see ... oh. Another thing is music. I try to put together a playlist of something that will go with the theme. The ranch has all the equipment you'll need and Dustin can work with you on it."

"That sounds easy. I can get Paige to do that when she gets back." Taryn smiled at Dustin as she said this and he grinned.

They talked about other details, until Taryn felt comfortable with what she needed to do. By that time Heather admitted she was feeling tired so everyone wished her well and ended the call. Bobby went back to work in the kitchen while Jesse talked to Taryn about the usual dining setup for the barbeque.

Taryn suddenly perked up, a slow grin lighting up her face.

"Dustin, before you bring Paige back from town, would you have her call me? There's something I'd like her to pick up, an idea I have about the decorations."

"Sure, but can't you just tell me now?"

"Nope. It's a surprise," Taryn said mischievously.

Jesse and Dustin exchanged worried looks.

"What's the matter boys? Don't you trust me?" She raised her eyebrows at Jesse with the last question. He gave her a knowing smile and said, "Yeah, I guess I do."

After they'd left Bobby's office, Taryn made a pretext of needing to take a quick look at the patio space so she could visualize what she had in mind in the way of decorations, promising to meet Jesse later. When he and Dustin were safely out of sight, she made a beeline back to Bobby.

"Knock, knock. Can I talk to you a bit about what I was thinking for the barbecue?"

"Sure, little lady. Come on in," Bobby said with a smile. "I could tell you had something cookin' there and I'd be happy to help."

Taryn briefly outlined her plans and Bobby enthusiastically agreed to fit at least part of the cuisine to match. He warned her though that the main course was not to be tampered with— this was a barbeque after all. She acquiesced, thoroughly pleased that Bobby was willing to assist.

She started to get up to go, but paused and sat back down when she saw the solemn look on Bobby's face..

"Taryn, a lot of Jesse's sadness has lifted since you've been here. You're really good for him. I hope you know that."

Taryn blushed, pleased. "Thank you Bobby, for saying so." She touched his arm briefly but affectionately. "Thanks for taking the time to talk to me. And do *not* tell Jesse what my plan is. I really want it to be a surprise."

"Don't you worry about that darlin'."

Taryn left Bobby and went straight to her cabin to start planning what she wanted for the barbeque surprise. She got so engrossed in the details, she completely skipped lunch, and barely made it to the movie. Ichika handed her a bowl of popcorn as she plopped into a chair.

Shortly after the movie ended, Paige and Dustin returned. Taryn rushed to meet her friend, grabbing her in a big hug.

"Derek. How is he? What happened?"

"Some dimwit driver was texting, texting! on the highway and crossed the center line. Smashed the hell out of Derek's car. He was really lucky he only had a broken leg and lots of bruises. The break was bad enough they had to do surgery to put a plate in. God you should see the x-ray of it—gave me the willies. But recovery should be pretty much a hundred percent. It'll take six months though. No skiing this season."

"I'm sure he'll miss that. Still I'm so glad he's going to be okay. How are you doing?" Taryn was feeling a bit guilty she hadn't been with her friend during this ordeal.

Paige took a deep breath. "Much better now. God I was so shaken when I got the call. Well, you know how it is when your kid gets hurt."

Did she ever. Taryn knew Paige was talking about that awful day two years ago when Amy had a ruptured ovarian cyst. Out for one of their frequent girls' lunches, they'd had no idea what was going on inside her; Amy just suddenly doubled over in pain. By the time they got her looked at in the emergency room she'd lost half her blood internally and had to be rushed to surgery. Taryn shuddered.

Paige dropped her voice to a whisper. "So, you and Jesse. Dustin told me you have something going but I want full details. Spill, girl." Paige was never one to beat about the bush.

"Let's go back to your cabin first. The lodge here is a bit open ..."

Chapter

13

Once Paige had her things somewhat put away, she plopped down on the bed and gave Taryn an expectant grin. "Go."

"Well, we went out for a ride on the trail and got caught in a freak snowstorm ..."

Paige interrupted her, "No, no. Get to the good stuff."

Taryn sighed. "Okay, we talked a lot and had sex a lot and then we got rescued by snowmobiles." She chuckled at the crestfallen, then pouty expression on Paige's face.

"Seriously, we had some incredible talks. Jesse has done a bunch of spiritual conferences and he knows so much about things I've never even thought about. He helped me see the whole divorce thing in an entirely new way."

The casualness Taryn had in her voice when she'd said the word "divorce" astounded Paige. This had been a very, very difficult subject for three years now.

"What new way?"

"So obviously Wyatt wanted out. Jesse helped me see that actually I wanted out too, that I really did know the marriage wasn't good for me anymore."

"Finally," Paige exhaled. "I was wondering how much longer it would take for you to get that."

Taryn's eyes widened in surprise. "What do you mean? You felt that way—that I should get out?"

"Of course. Seemed pretty clear cut to me. You were determined to pretend everything was great so I couldn't say anything to you, but when your guard was down I could see how miserable you were."

Taryn was stunned. So everyone knew but her? "Good grief, how stupid have I been?"

"Don't be too hard on yourself. Jeez, from the outside it looked like you had it all. I don't blame you for wanting to hold onto the dream." She wasn't sure she should ask this, but ... "Did he say anything about Wyatt's cheating?"

Taryn brightened. "That was the most amazing thing. He thinks that because I wouldn't leave, Wyatt had to take that on. That the cheating was basically about making a way to end it all."

"Sounds just like something a guy would say, a convenient excuse," Paige said in a plainly disgusted tone. While her lifestyle was certainly not settled on one man, she was always careful to make that clear to the men she dated. Playing around on a partner who expected monogamy was not okay with her.

"Ah, but this is the amazing part, Paige. Jesse explained to me about the secret, unconscious contracts people—especially married people—make with each other. It's a whole different level of looking at things. He says that because both of us wanted out, but I wouldn't make the first move, Wyatt had to. And that at this really deep unconscious level we both agreed to this. His having an affair gave him a new spark in life; my not having been the one to cheat or leave let me continue to be the 'good girl,' protected that image for me. It was a win-win."

The perplexed expression on her friend's face almost had Taryn laughing. "Huh? You lost me at secret contracts. Sounds a bit out there to me."

"Actually it's not, at least not so much as you are thinking right now. Everyone has unspoken agreements with other people. You and me for example."

"Say what? We don't have secrets. We talk all the time," Paige interjected.

"Yeah, but. You're the zany one who makes all these crazy plans to go to a dude ranch—thank you very much by the way. We never really talked about how that role would fall to you, and that I would follow. Remember our first night in the dorm? You decided we should go skinny-dipping in the pool at two a.m.? Right then we made our agreement, without words. What Jesse was talking about is essentially the same thing, just on a much deeper level."

Paige was astounded. "Let me get this straight. You *agreed* to let Wyatt cheat on you? Girl, I've been through the last three years with you. That's ridiculous."

"Actually, it's not Paige. And remember, that agreement was unconscious, Jesse says at a soul level. Doesn't mean it didn't still hurt, to be cheated on and left. But something had to be done to get us both free. Like you said—we were miserable."

"It still seems preposterous to me. Why do you believe him?"

"Because I can *feel* it Paige. When he said it my head wanted to resist at first, but as it began to sink in I could feel how true it was." Seeing the skeptical look on Paige's face, she explained. "Remember when Derek was born? And you saw him for the first time. Did anyone need to convince you that you loved him? Hell no. You just *knew* you loved him; it was automatic, went all the way through you, no thought or decision needed. Well it felt like that when Jesse showed me how to see the end of my marriage differently."

Paige nodded, and shrugged.

Taryn continued. "Think about it, how smoothly the divorce went. Neither of us dragging each other through the mud, neither trying to take advantage of the other. Really, really deep down the love and respect were still there."

She choked up, thinking about what she'd just said. Chills, energetic, ran through her as the next realization fully hit her at a deeper level. Internally, the tumblers clicked one by one, until at last the key turned in the lock and a door swung wide open.

"OMG, Paige, that whole victim thing just completely fell away. The splitting up wasn't something that was done to me; I was part of it; I agreed to it. Wyatt and I did it together." Her face registered shock, her eyes delight.

Even Paige, who still barely understood what Taryn was saying, had to admit her friend had radically changed. She felt the maturity, the serene acceptance of this woman who, until three days ago, had felt scorned and beaten.

"Wow, Taryn," said Paige admiringly. "I'm happy for you. Feels like you're more alive now than you've been for ..., well, for many years."

"I am. I'm so grateful to Jesse, for all he taught me." Taryn was glowing. Quietly, mostly to herself, she added, "Wow. Maybe Jesse should be a teacher, do for others what he did for me."

Paige reflected. "You two must have had some really long conversations. I'm having a hard time wrapping my head around that one—Jesse hasn't really seemed like much of a talker."

Taryn considered, remembering her first impression of him as walled off, and had to agree. "No, he's not, or hasn't been, in his role as host of the ranch. But when he's not having to play host, and he's getting real, he has a lot to say. Especially when we were sharing about our lives, the insights of how things happened, Jesse was great to talk to."

"Yes, about you and Jesse. Apart from the talking, what's going on with you two?"

"Told you already we connected on the physical level too. Yum and a half," she said dreamily. "I haven't felt that way, ever. Probably because it was more than just physical really. Paige he's so—present. Compassionate, interested. And you know how we talked before about this wall he has? He let that down, let me in too. I think I'm falling for him."

Paige shook her head. "Lordy, I leave you alone for two days …" She took Taryn's hand and squeezed it. "This is the best news ever." Her eyes crinkled with the wide grin spreading over her face.

"So where do you think it will go from here? Have you talked about it?"

Taryn sighed pensively. "I have no idea, and no, we haven't. I mean until this morning it didn't seem like we were even going to be able to be together much down here at the ranch. But Dustin says everyone already knows." She grinned, remembering. "Actually I wish you could have been here at breakfast. Jesse planted a big kiss on me and everyone cheered. It was kind of cool."

"Yeah, Dustin told me about that. I do wish I'd been here. Bet Sparkle boy was pissed though."

"Have to admit I wasn't exactly focused on him," she said with eyebrows raised. "I …"

The thought was broken by the unmistakable sounds of the dinner bell.

"Guess we'll talk more later, okay."

Taryn felt contented as she sat down at her place for dinner and looked around the room at the other guests she had come to like so well. Kathy and Mark sat to her right; they were chatting happily, but softly, about something that was clearly just between them. Ichika and Kaito sat across from her, their arms around each other, so in love. Paige had not yet sat down. She was still flirting with Dustin by the kitchen door, and the sound of their laughter brought Bobby out to see what was up. When he saw his ranch buddy so enthralled, he smiled and winked at Taryn before going back to work. Tadao and Eric were engrossed in a techie conversation she could only catch hints of. They'd become buds too, once Eric got Tadao onto Sparkle. When Jesse walked into the room and glanced at her lovingly, Taryn's heart was full.

Of course, everyone wanted to know all about Taryn's budding relationship with Jesse. She'd left early at breakfast to confer with Bobby and Heather about the barbeque—less than twenty-four hours away now—so she'd barely made it to the movie, and no one but Paige had talked to her since. Taryn had to admit to them that something was going on, while still emphasizing how new and uncertain it all was at this point. Her words were not enough to satisfy curious minds, but it was all she could do.

Then she got very serious as she said, "Look, guys, I really need you to promise me something. You all know about my attachment to Jesse, and that's cool while it's just us here. But at the barbeque—there will be people from town and guests from B&Bs attending. It's so important that they not know about Jesse and me."

Eric broke in. "I don't see why not. What's the big deal?"

Taryn could hear the flash of anger in his voice, and almost responded in kind. Then the patience she'd learned as a mother took over.

"Jesse has a reputation to protect; he can't become known as the guy who hits on his ranch guests. It could ruin his business. If he had a wife, well, that would obviously be different. But we don't know what we are yet, how far this relationship will go."

Taryn almost went white when it finally registered that she'd said the word "wife." The thought that she could one day wind up as Jesse's wife had not even come close to being on her radar yet. It sent her emotions swirling.

Kathy knew immediately what was happening with her friend and reached out to gently touch her arm as Eric continued with his confrontational questions.

"Won't everyone know anyway, the way you two act with each other? I bet those long kisses like this morning will be a dead giveaway." There was more than just a little bitterness in his voice.

Taryn regained her composure. "We've already talked about this, and we're going to be cordial but somewhat distant tomorrow. Please, please be respectful and don't tell anyone."

She looked around the table and everyone nodded, even Eric, however reluctantly.

"Thank you so much. Now I have a lot of work still to do so I'll be on my way."

Eric caught up with Taryn just as she walked out the door. He looked surprisingly awkward.

"Taryn, can I ask you something?"

"Of course, Eric. What is it?"

He looked so uncomfortable, obviously unsure how to form the question. Finally he blurted out, "Why him and not me?" His eyes went wide, just before they dropped to the ground.

Seeing his angst, she decided to be gentle with him. "You know, you're a lot like my ex-husband."

"Oh, I get it." He turned to move away.

"Wait. Eric. That's not a bad thing. What you have in common is a very confident take-charge way of being that expects people to fall in line after you. When I was younger, and met my husband, I loved that energy. I was happy to follow. For a long time he was a good leader in our relationship. But I'm older now and I want something different. I need a gentler man, one who will listen to me, be a more equal partner with me."

Eric's pained expression eased a bit. "Okay."

There was still a hint of confusion on his face though.

"I get the feeling you're not sure you understand what I just said."

Eric shook his head.

"You're a powerful man, Eric. I could tell that when you walked up to the van at the airport. You're the founder, the CEO of Sparkle, a large company. That took a lot of work and dedication. And imagination, to come up with such an app. Only someone with a lot of drive and ability to command the people who work for you could accomplish that. I respect that. But I've already played the background person in a relationship with a powerful man. I don't want to be a follower anymore. I want to walk beside my man, not behind him. Can you see what I mean?"

He thought for a second. "Like you want your own career?"

Taryn smiled and tried to find the words that would make sense to him. "Yes, essentially. Even if it wasn't being the CEO of a company, but teaching in my own yoga studio. Or even just doing volunteer work. But my own work, not just supporting his."

"Oh," said Eric.

Taryn could see things were beginning to register with him.

"Eric you just need to find someone who matches you better, someone who will be happy letting you take the lead. Do you understand now?"

"I guess so." He set his mouth in a thin line of disappointment, but he held out his hand to her. "You're something special, Taryn. Thanks for telling me all that."

She smiled and gently laid her hand on his arm. "You're welcome, Eric. Good luck."

He turned and looked back over his shoulder as he walked away, "Still think you need to set up a Sparkle account ..."

Taryn laughed.

Jesse had been holding back, watching Taryn and Eric talking. He realized with a shock that he was jealous, seeing her touch Eric's arm. The feeling was so distant, so unfamiliar. And until it came rushing in, he hadn't understood just how much he really cared for Taryn. It frightened him a little, until he remembered how it was to be with her in the cabin—intimate, comfortable, alive. He walked up behind her and put his arms around her waist. Before she could turn around he pressed his warm lips to her neck.

"Ummm. You do know how to say hi to a girl." She responded with a soft kiss on the mouth.

"Taryn," he hesitated, just for a moment unsure whether this would be moving too fast. But their time was short. "I want you to spend the night with me, in my house."

She gasped. She knew this was an unprecedented tear in his protective shield.

"Jesse, are you sure? This feels like a big step for you."

"Yes. It is, you're right. My house is my sanctuary, so to speak, and I've never invited anyone up before. This week, this time with you, has been full of firsts." He looked longingly into her eyes. "I want you in my home. I want you in my bed. I want the closeness we had in the cabin. Is that too much to ask of you?"

She gently stroked his cheek, kissed him again. "No. I think I would like that very much."

He took her hand and brought it to his lips. Without another word he led her up the hill.

Jesse's home looked exactly as she would have expected. Warm and full of soft color, it was every bit the sanctuary he'd said it was. Rustic, but not so pronounced as the lodge, the rich wood and rough stone, worn leather and diffuse lighting immediately gave her a feeling of peace and calm. Just like its owner.

"Jesse, I love it!" she gushed, her eyes sparkling. "It's beautiful."

"I'm so glad you like it," he said, flushing slightly. He was surprised to realize how important it was to him that she feel comfortable here. And even more surprised to discover that it felt like she belonged here, in this space that had been so private just to him.

"Would you like a glass of wine, while I show you around?"

"Yes, that would be great."

He crossed to the kitchen and poured the wine. They went

through the living room, study, screened in porch with its view of the mountains behind the house, the small guest room. The tour included stories of the ranch's previous owner and builder of the house, and the history of it. When they reached the master bedroom, Taryn found herself immersed in the energy and presence of Jesse, a feeling so serene and sensual she felt it wrap around her like a deep hug. She nearly dropped her wine glass.

Instead, she turned to him, her eyes full of desire.

He responded instantly. He took the glass from her hand and set it on the dresser next to his. Slowly he removed her blouse, unzipped her jeans. Eyes locked on his, she did the same for him. They stood then, naked, just taking each other in with their eyes.

He reached out to her, lightly brushing her cheek, then ever so slowly trailed his fingers down her neck, her chest, and circled her breast. Suddenly she burst out laughing.

He froze.

"Oh God, Jesse, this is how one of the love scenes started in my favorite steamy romance novel. I can't believe I'm living this out."

She threw her arms around him, pulled him tightly to her.

"And you are so, so much better. Jesse, you've made me come alive again."

She pushed him to the bed. Straddling him, she watched his face, felt every twitch of him and brought them both to the brink and away again, extending the pleasure for them both. Finally neither could hold back and they came hard and quick, explosions of passion.

They lay side by side, panting.

"My God, woman. What you do to me."

Then in almost a whisper, "I love you, Taryn."

Chapter
14

Her first awareness next morning was the feeling of Jesse gently stroking her arm, his warm body spooning hers. In the moments between sleep and wakefulness a smile touched her lips as she realized she was home. With a shock, her eyes went wide open. *No! What? Oh my God.* A tremor ran through her as she tried to shake off the thoughts she could not yet deal with, that Jesse's home could feel like it was hers too.

Jesse felt her move, and his fingers found their way to her breast. That she could handle, and she turned to embrace him, kissing him with clear intent. His fingers slowly wandered south, between her legs as she gently stroked him. Hungry for each other, they made love with an intensity that carried them both quickly over the edge.

Finally catching his breath, Jesse rolled onto his side and propped himself up on one elbow.

"I love making love to you, Taryn. And what I wouldn't give to spend all day in bed with you. Being with you is the most amazing thing I've ever felt." He sighed. "But I have work to do, and the bell for breakfast will be ringing soon."

"Oh, no. But I don't want breakfast. I just want you," said Taryn, moving her hips to his.

Jesse had to control the urge to make love with her again. "Darling, we have to talk."

His tone was serious; she moved away, uncertain.

"Taryn we haven't talked about what's to happen next. You're supposed to leave tomorrow. I don't want you to. I want you to stay, here, with me."

"What? What do you mean, stay?" The word sent her into turmoil. Hope and fear filled her head. She hadn't even let herself think beyond the last day of her week here. Everything had been moving so quickly—from not even wanting a new man in her life to this amazing intense connection with Jesse. She was barely making it from moment to moment, and now he was talking about a future?

"I mean I want you to stay here, not go back to Seattle. I know that's a lot to ask of you. You have a life there. And I have no idea where this, us, will go. But I'd like us to give it a chance."

He paused, to give her time to speak, but she couldn't yet.

"What I was thinking, hoping really, is that maybe you could stay here for a few more weeks. We could find out what it would be like. Find out what our feelings really are. Find out how it would be to live together. Figure it out from there."

She was still silent, and it was killing him. He was so afraid she would say no, crush the budding love in his heart. He held his breath.

"Jesse. Oh, Jesse. I don't know what to say. A week ago I didn't even want to get involved with anybody. This is moving so fast. I have no idea how to answer you."

She caught the look of dejection on his face and hastily added,

"That doesn't mean my answer would be no. Jesse, I really care for you, you have to know that. I have cherished the time with you too. And, this is a big ask. Please, I need some time to think ..."

"Of course. I do understand." He took a shaky breath. "Perhaps, for right now, we could both just use some breakfast."

Gratefully, she nodded, and kissed him tenderly. They held each other close for a few more minutes, then reluctantly got up and dressed to return to the outside world.

⌒〜⌒

"Hey, Dustin said he saw you coming out of Jesse's house. Did you spend the night with him?" whispered Paige as she slid into her seat at the breakfast table.

Taryn nodded slowly, her eyes downcast. Paige was about to question her further, but plates of food, along with Kathy and Mark, arrived and she thought it best to wait. So she struck up a conversation with the others. Taryn joined in from time to time, though it was clear she was quite distracted. Paige was beginning to wonder just how bad the night with Jesse had been. As soon as she could, she whisked her friend aside and told her to get to her cabin.

"All right, what gives? You just spent the night with your new dreamboat cowboy and you look like death warmed over."

Taryn broke down in tears, sat heavily on the bed. "Paige. He asked me to stay with him." Her eyes looked pleadingly at her trusted friend as if to say, "What the hell am I going to do?"

Paige let out a breath. "Jeez. I have to admit I didn't see that coming. What did you tell him?"

"I didn't. Not yet. I got as far as saying that's a big ask when we got interrupted by breakfast. He looked horrible when I left him."

She paused, remembering the pained expression in his eyes as they'd walked out his door. "He wants me to stay for a few weeks, to find out what we are and where it could go."

"Stay here? Seriously? Taryn, have you even told Amy and Josh about him?"

Taryn shook her head slowly so Paige continued.

"How could you think about staying when you haven't talked to them? You know how cracked up they both were when you and Wyatt split. How are they going to feel about some new man in your life?"

"Oh God, I hadn't thought about that. This is all happening so fast. I hardly know which end is up."

"What about all the work you do for the gallery? Weren't you supposed to start on that new exhibit when we get back? Have you thought about that?"

Again Taryn shook her head. She looked shyly at her friend. "Paige, he told me he loves me."

"*Loves* you? This is crazy fast. Are you sure you believe him?" Paige was becoming a bit worried.

"I don't know," she said meekly. "Now that you ask. It seems impossible, I mean five days ago we hadn't even met." She stopped when she remembered Jesse's voice as he'd told her. "It felt real when he said it."

Suddenly facing the possibility of being abandoned, essentially, by this friend who had been a constant in her life for decades, sent Paige into a tailspin. "And what happens after a few weeks and you decide to make a go of it? Are you supposed to leave Seattle, leave your kids, leave your life there to come live in f'ing Colorado on a ranch?" Her voice was nearly hysterical as she said, "How could you?"

Taryn was shocked at the intensity of her friend's tone. They'd never had a real fight before. But unable to get past her own sense of panic, she could do nothing to allay Paige's fears.

"I don't know what will happen. Honestly, I don't know much of anything right now. I haven't had time to think this through, or even get my own feelings straight. I think I just need to be alone now. I'm sorry, Paige."

She got up to leave, go to her own cabin. Paige stood silent as a mournful look passed between them. Taryn turned and walked out.

Paige was miserable. Stunned at Taryn's news and the possibilities it presented. And equally upset by the way she'd just treated her dearest friend, yelling at her instead of supporting her, helping her work through the difficult decision she faced.

She decided to drop the plans she'd made to go shopping in town with the others and phoned the spa for a massage and body wrap. As she left to walk to the appointment, she spotted Jesse walking toward Taryn's cabin.

With a grim look she told him, "I wouldn't if I were you. Girl needs some space."

She walked on by without waiting for a response.

Taryn collapsed on her bed as soon as she walked in her cabin. She let the tears come in waves. Tears for thoughts of leaving Jesse, for staying with him but leaving her home and family and friends, her life. Paige's reaction had brought it into sharp focus, what she would be sacrificing to stay.

How in the world am I going to tell Amy and Josh about this? That

I've met someone? That I might be in love with him? That I might stay with him? In—for crying out loud—Colorado? This whole thing is nuts. What about my condo? All the obligations I have in Seattle? Paige? And Wyatt? What the hell would I say to him now, after all Jesse's helped me see?

And yet, Jesse. No one had opened her up the way he had. His gentle strength, his wisdom, his sensitive lovemaking—how could she even think about letting that disappear from her life? Her heart cried out at the very thought.

She sat up and dried her face. Taking deep breaths to calm herself, she tried to bring some rationality to the situation.

You're running way too far ahead here. Take this one small step at a time. He wants you to stay for a few weeks. To find out what's what. That's doable. Just an extension of a fun (and very sexy) vacation. I do know it's what I really want. Any other decisions will have to come after, if it comes to that at all. She took another deep breath. *Okay, I think I can handle this.*

She checked her face in the mirror, carefully reapplying her makeup. Then she stood gazing at her reflection for a long time, getting solidly in touch with the woman behind the eyes. She remembered looking at herself like this as she was packing for the week, how she'd felt so in limbo between her old life and the unknown future. That had made her feel ill at ease then, but now there was an internal strength and a confidence that she could deal with whatever might be coming her way. It was reflected most in her eyes, the ones she had seen such melancholy and doubt in before. Now there was a clarity beginning to show, and a resolve. She smiled confidently at herself. *Time to find Jesse and Paige, tell them what I want.*

Taryn caught Jesse just as they were entering the lodge for lunch. He was ecstatic when she said she'd stay for three weeks. He grabbed her in a passionate embrace, kissing her with a ferocity he didn't know he had in him, completely forgetting his earlier warning to Taryn to keep the PDA down.

"Taryn, darling, you have no idea how happy that makes me!" His tone subdued to one of serious gratitude. "I do know how big a decision this was for you. Thank you, for giving us a chance." With a twinkle in his eye he added, "I promise to make it worth your while." He gave her a full body hug.

"You'd better," she teased.

"How about we move some of your things up to my place after we get the decorations done. You can keep your cabin—no one else has reserved it—in case you need some time to yourself. Does that work for you?"

She thought for a moment. He wanted her to live in his home, be a constant part of his life, in a way she hadn't shared her life with anyone for a long time. Was she ready for that? But he'd offered her own space should she want it. "Yes, Jesse. Wow. Moving in together. It's a lot to take in."

"It is for me too, Taryn. I've never even invited anyone inside my house before. And yet, when you walked in, I knew you belonged there too. I hope in time you can feel that way as well."

"I do too. Can I tell you a secret? When I woke up this morning, in your arms, I had the flash of a feeling that I was home. Shook me a bit then, but now ..."

He took her hand, raised it to his lips. He could not find words to express his heart in the moment, so he tried to convey all he was feeling with his eyes. Taryn smiled happily.

"Okay, mister. I have work to do. All those decorations for the barbeque tonight aren't going to put themselves up. Paige has been keeping them in her cabin so I've got to go get her, then we'll meet you on the patio."

"You're finally going to let me see what they are? It's time for the big reveal?" He laughed and followed her out the door.

Taryn ran into Paige just as she was leaving the spa. Instantly they were in each other's arms, in the sisterly hug so familiar to them both.

"Oh God, Taryn, I'm so sorry. What was I thinking? You finally find a man, who makes you happy, and instead of being thrilled for you I say such shitty things. Can you ever forgive me?"

Taryn pulled away just enough so she could look Paige in the face. "Are you kidding, girl? Already done. You just brought up things I hadn't thought of before. And have decided not to try to think about yet. I've told Jesse I'll stay for three weeks. After that—who knows? If I start making plans any further out, I'll go crazy."

"Three weeks. I think I can handle not having you in Seattle for that long." Paige pouted doubtfully. "And that sounds like it will give you a good chance to find out what you really want. Taryn, I really am so happy for you. Jesse feels like he's really good for you."

"Oh, he so is," Taryn said contentedly. "And you know what? This whole thing, and the questions you asked about how Josh and Amy will take it, have made me realize that I really do need to stop caring so much about what others think. This is my life. They're a huge part of it, for sure, but so is Jesse now. I have to do what's best for me. It's time to step up."

Soberly, Paige said, "You're right, of course. However much we might miss having you in Seattle with us, if you belong here with

Jesse, then so be it." A slow smile spread over her face. "You're starting to stand up for what *you* want, Taryn. Finally. I'm so proud of you."

She reached out to hug her again. "Come on. I have something I need to tell you too."

Arm in arm they walked to Paige's cabin. When they got inside, they got distracted a bit looking over the items Paige had brought back from town for the barbeque decorating. She'd done well, with Dustin's help. Taryn was excited to see how they would all turn out. Then she turned her focus back to Paige.

"So what's going on with you?"

"Well I guess you could say I've had a bit of a change myself. Between Derek and Dustin—hey they both start with D, interesting—I'm starting to feel my life needs to go in a new direction."

Taryn was curious. "That's great. Isn't it?"

"It is. When I was in the hospital with Derek and Charlotte, it hit me. Derek needs to be his own man now. There's a new woman in his life and I really think they're good together. I need to let him go." She paused.

"Wow, that is a big change for you," Taryn said quietly.

Paige nodded. "You know the bond between Derek and I has always been so strong. Sometimes I think Jack was only in my life to plant the seed, so to speak. But now bonds have to change. You know how you said you could just feel that what Jesse told you about how you and Wyatt ended was true? Well I guess that's how it happened for me in that hospital room. I could not have put into words then, but I could feel that something was ... releasing. Does that make any sense?"

Taryn reached out to take Paige's hand. "Of course it does. Jesse would call it an energetic shift." She smiled as she realized she'd adopted a new vocabulary. "Derek's allegiance has always been to you, and now it's gone to Charlotte. Release is a good word for it." She grinned. "And that leaves you a 'free radical,' so to speak."

"Interesting way to put it, but I think you're right. Derek and I will always be close—how could we not be? But now we have our own lives to live somehow."

A slow smile spread across Taryn's face. "This is so wonderful! Especially since you seem to be really settled with it."

"I am. I really am." Paige nodded, eyes bright. "You know, I tried to call you, tell you about it, but the call wouldn't go through. Guess that must have been while you were up in the cabin."

"Yeah, sorry. My phone wouldn't work at all, and even Jesse's could only do texting. Damn, I would have loved to talk with you." A trace of sadness crossed Taryn's face, then faded as she smiled at Paige. "Honestly, it always felt to me that this was inevitable. I'm so glad to know you've accepted it. Nothing can truly replace the relationship a mother and son have, and you'll always have it. I remember how hard it was when Josh moved out. 'Bout killed me. Well, you saw it. And yet—the pride, knowing he was ready to make his own way in life. I can see that you're feeling that way now about Derek."

Paige looked almost shy. "There's something else. Dustin has shown me that I might at last be capable and ready to take on a longer term relationship."

Taryn interrupted her in excitement. "Oh, Paige, you and Dustin! Are you falling in love?"

"No, I don't think so. It's different with us than with you and Jesse," Paige said. "We're not in love. More along the lines of 'extreme like.' But you know, being with Dustin has made me start thinking about *really* being with someone again. Derek is moving out in his own life, with a woman to share it. It's like Derek is showing me that we can both be attached to others, and Dustin is showing me that too.

Even though I don't have any idea where Dustin and I could go, as a relationship. He's just sort of opened the door."

"It might just be that your letting go of Derek is what's made it possible for you to be open to having another man in your life."

Paige considered. "I think you're right. I hadn't thought of it that way, but it makes sense."

"That's so great." Taryn reached out to hug her friend. "I'm so happy for you."

"Thanks. Interesting week, huh? Who'd have thought we'd wind up with *cowboys*? Let's go decorate for the barbecue, finish it off in style."

Chapter
15

Though they skipped lunch to do it, decorating went quickly, both because Taryn had planned well and because Jesse and Dustin were enthusiastic about the theme she'd chosen. When they finished, Taryn asked Jesse if he had time to talk for a while.

"Sure, I'll make time for you. Maybe we should go up to my place?"

They wandered slowly up to his cabin, arms wrapped around each other's waists. Just touching in this comfortable way was so intimate and serene that they were silent until they walked inside.

Jesse poured two glasses of wine, handed one to Taryn and sat beside her on his couch.

"Cheers." He raised his glass, lightly touched hers. "Now what did you want to talk about?"

"You picked that movie, *The Wife*, on purpose, didn't you?"

"Yes. I thought it might be interesting for you in light of some of the things we discussed at the hunters' cabin."

"It was. Especially the ending. There's something about it I can't quite put my finger on. But it has to do with secret contracts doesn't it?"

"It does, for me. Actually I think the ending can be interpreted, if you will, several ways. His heart attack, and the timing of it, could just be coincidental—that's the common way of looking at it. Or maybe he really believed she would leave him and he couldn't stand to live without her so he left her first."

"Yes, I can see both of those. Except he couldn't have just made himself have a heart attack, could he?"

"No. When I say he left, I mean that his soul opted out. Unlikely that he could have or would have consciously chosen to make himself die. His soul however has the power to make that choice, to leave. You see that with older couples who have been together for a long, long time. One dies, and within weeks the other does too. Not by suicide, I don't mean that. The soul makes the choice not to stay here without the mate."

"Oh, I kind of remember hearing something about that."

"Apparently it's not uncommon. Heard it from a doctor friend of mine. But going back to the movie. Another possibility is that he knew she wanted out, needed out, and also knew she might not be able to actually do it on her own. So he gave her the out by leaving first. He set her free."

Taryn drew in a breath. "Like Wyatt did for me." She slumped down onto the pillows behind her. "Oh Jesse ..."

He took her hand, just held it while she took it all in. Finally she was able to speak again.

"When I think of how hard the divorce was on him, how many years we both spent being so unhappy ... because I didn't leave. So many years of me just following him, even though he was ready to go. Years wasted ..."

"Wait. You're talking like what your life has been was somehow wrong—like you should have been stronger, or more career minded, or that being a corporate wife and mother was somehow less than what you should have been. Don't invalidate your life. There is great value in all of what you did. Supporting Wyatt in his business—he could never have gotten so far without you. Because of you he was able to build a comfortable life for you and your children. And being home gave your kids the stability they needed to grow into strong people able to handle this world. Add in your volunteer work and you've got yourself a very respectable contribution to life. So don't put it down. Don't minimize your life to this point."

She dropped her head, whispered, "Thank you."

He lifted her chin and forced her to meet his penetrating gaze. With his eyes, and the slight smile on his lips, he conveyed his admiration for her.

"And, Taryn. That was one phase of your life. That needed to come to an end so you could move on to the next one. At a very deep level it's as simple as that. From life's point of view there's no *blame* here, for you or for Wyatt. The divorce was just what needed to be, for both of you to move on to the next phase. Can you feel that, just a little?"

Taryn's eyes widened as she distanced herself from the emotion of it all, saw the overview of her life. If you left out all the messy details and just looked at the basic plot line it all became so much clearer. She felt the truth of what Jesse said, even without having a complete understanding of why it had had to be so.

"It really does help to see it on the screen. To see how it plays out from a distance, in other people's lives. It's amazing, isn't it, what people do for each other?" Taryn said with eyes full of wonder.

"It is," Jesse said. "Look what you've done for me—opened my heart, in a way I thought would never happen again. You're a very wise and special person."

She opened her mouth to protest, but Jesse stopped her.

"No, you don't get to deny it anymore. When we were in the cabin and you started to use anger as a defense, you caught right away what you were doing. You taught me about what 'trust' really means, and you learned that from your own life experiences. You've moved away from feeling like a victim in your divorce. You're the very definition of wisdom, my dear."

She stared at him for a minute. *My God, could he be right? That I am capable of being wise?* She thought back to the weeks before coming to the ranch, to the day when Amy moved out and Wyatt made his unwelcome appearance. She felt what it had been like to let him walk over her as he had so many times, felt again what it had been like to be the "woman scorned." *I really have come a long way since then. My whole world is different ... I'm different.* Her eyes registered acceptance, then deep appreciation.

Jesse leaned forward, kissing her softly on the cheek. Instantly her arms were around him, pulling him into a full embrace.

Eagerly she asked, "Do we have time, before the barbeque?"

Taryn and Paige had saved their fanciest new cowgirl dresses for this last night of their dude ranch week, and they spent plenty of time with their hair and makeup to look especially nice for Jesse and Dustin. Dressing up had always been a favorite for these two. They'd planned to get to the lodge early, to be sure everything was set up as intended. When they walked out onto the patio, Dustin's mouth dropped open and Paige did a little happy twirl. Jesse had to play it cool, but the look in his eyes spoke volumes.

The vans from town, with the B&B guests who'd signed up for the barbeque, arrived early too. There were twenty-two of them—fewer than normal, but it was September and the end of the season. Jesse welcomed them all and showed them to the patio.

Taryn would never forget the looks of joy on the faces of Ichika, Kaito and Tadao as they walked out onto the patio that evening. Japanese lanterns of various colors hung from wires, crisscrossing through the space, providing a soft glow. In the center of each table were bonsai trees, borrowed from the nursery in town. Majestic orchids stood tall in vases on the appetizer table. Bobby had gone all out finding recipes for gyoza, tempura and yakitori appetizers. Place settings at the guest tables included carved wooden chopsticks and starched napkins folded like flying cranes. Dustin had even managed to find some popular Japanese tunes to play, and as Tadao recognized the song coming through the speakers, he began singing along with it.

Ichika rushed to Taryn and bowed, then embraced her with a hug, uncharacteristic for her normally reserved nature.

"Oh Taryn, and Paige, how exquisite!"

Taryn smiled broadly. "I'm so glad you like it, Ichika. Paige and I just wanted to honor our new Japanese friends. We've really enjoyed getting to know you this week."

Kaito walked up then and took Ichika's hand. She dropped her head shyly, still not used to being free to be open with her affection for him when there were so many people around.

"Thank you too, Taryn, for making it safe for Kaito and me to stop hiding our love. It has made us realize that we should not be ashamed of how we feel about each other. We have decided that when we return to work, we will tell management about our relationship and if they will not allow us to continue there as a couple, then one of us will find work somewhere else." She glanced lovingly at Kaito, who said, "We want to get married, and have a family."

Taryn smiled gently at her friends. "I know that must have been a hard decision to make. It takes courage to stand up for yourself when there are such strict rules in place. I hope you will let me know what happens."

"I will. And I hope you also tell me what happens with you and Jesse." Ichika smiled and Taryn blushed.

"Definitely. Shall we sit down? I know Bobby worked hard on this meal and I can't wait to see what he prepared."

Just as she uttered the last word, Bobby and his staff of servers came out onto the patio bearing huge platters of barbeque ribs, chicken and brisket. Baskets of giant baked potatoes and pots of baked beans were set beside them on the buffet serving tables, where condiments and salad had been placed earlier. The smells were tantalizing, and as Taryn caught Bobby's eye, she gave him a thumbs up.

Before taking her place at the table, Paige walked up to Jesse and without a word, hugged him tight. Shocked, he patted her back until she let him go.

"Jesse. I really want to thank you for what you've done for Taryn. I don't understand half of what you told her, but she's so changed. Until this trip, and you, the word 'divorce' was strictly taboo. In fact we came here to get her mind off the date-that-shall-not-be-talked-about. Now ... well, I think she's moving past it. Thanks to you." Contrary to their last encounter, Paige's tone was friendly again.

Jesse relaxed and breathed a sigh of relief. "I'm happy to hear you say that, Paige. I know she had a pretty rough time there. But she's an amazing woman, and she's come a long way."

Well, she thinks it's all because of you. In fact she thinks you should start teaching other people too."

Jesse was startled. *Teach? Me? Could I?* He opened his mouth to respond, but couldn't think of anything to say.

"You know, to stay here with you for even three weeks is a big deal for her." She pouted. "You better not make me lose my friend, Jesse. I don't know what I'd do without her."

He shook his head. "No way. You two are too close for that to ever happen." An idea struck. "Hey. Why don't you stay too? I'm betting Dustin would like that, a lot." He grinned.

"Hummm, tempting as that is, I can't. I have to get back and be sure Derek is okay. But maybe I could come back in a couple weeks? See how things are going then?" Paige brightened, thinking about being with Dustin again.

"Sounds like a plan. Come here. Gimme another hug."

Kathy pulled a chair up next to Taryn just as dessert was served.

"Hey, I just heard the good news from Paige. You're staying here with Jesse?"

"Yes, I am. Just for three weeks; that's all that's planned on right now. Neither of us has any idea what we'll turn out to be at this point."

Kathy was bubbling with excitement. "Well let me tell you then, I have it all figured out. You'd be a great addition to this ranch. You can teach yoga classes for the guests. And with your event planning skills, you could help Jesse turn this place into a premier wedding destination." She added breathlessly, "How does that sound?"

Taryn was taken aback. Instantaneously she was both annoyed and intrigued. She knew Kathy's intentions were good, but ... "Wow you really do have my life planned out." Giving in to Kathy's enthusiasm, she smiled.

"Oh, sorry to just be blurting all that out. Wine you know. My tongue's a little loose right now." Kathy screwed up her face to demonstrate.

"Those are actually both great ideas. Wonder if Jesse would go for that. We'll have to see what happens ..."

When dinner was over and all the dishes cleared, Dustin put on one of the songs everyone had heard at the bar and announced that he would be leading the line dancing. Immediately Ichika, Kaito and Tadao jumped up, excited to practice the new steps they'd learned earlier in the week. Most of the other guests, even those from town, joined in while the staff quickly moved the dinner tables to the side of the room. Jesse gave Taryn a longing look but kept his distance. He still had a reputation to protect. Ichika, dancing close to Kaito, was sorry for her friend.

Even while careful about appearing too close, Dustin and Paige still managed to be in full swing. Kathy and Mark moved up beside them, laughing happily. The four of them knew all the steps and led the newbies in dance after dance. Even Eric hooked up with a young woman from Michigan and fell in line.

It was well after midnight when the last of them finally gave out and retired to bed.

Chapter
16

The tone was much more subdued at breakfast the next morning, the day they would all be leaving. Once again, several of the group were nursing hangovers. The main downer though was that none of them really wanted to go. Even though their time together had been short, in many ways they'd become close friends.

As they had that first evening, Kathy, Paige and Taryn sat close together so they could talk.

Paige broke the heavy silence. "So Kathy, I was serious about introducing you to galleries in Seattle. When you get home send me the files of those pics you showed me, and I'll start showing them to the people I know best."

"Wow, that would be great Paige. Thank you."

"Don't thank me just yet. After we've gotten some interest you could bring some of your paintings up and we'll make the rounds."

Kathy grinned from ear to ear. "Oh that sounds like fun. It would be so amazing just to see the Seattle art scene, even if my paintings don't get into galleries there."

"And you can stay with me—that should make it even more fun. If we're lucky Taryn will be back in town then too …" She turned to her friend. "You've got to come back sometimes you know."

Kathy was ecstatic. "This gets better by the minute! It would be a blast to get together again."

"It would indeed," chimed in Taryn.

Kathy's eyes widened. "You know what would be really great? Why don't we all come back here next year?" She looked at Ichika and Kaito, Tadao. "What do you guys think? It would be incredible to see each other again, get caught up with how our lives have gone. And Eric I bet your shrink would recommend it. You've mellowed out a lot since you first got here."

Eric snorted. "Well, I have to admit you're right about that. I know you all thought I spent way too much time on the phone while I was here, but it's nothing compared to how I am normally. It was kind of nice to be disconnected, relatively. I might even try horseback riding again."

Taryn and Paige held in a laugh, remembering his first experience.

Mark said, "Eric, I think that would be a very manly thing to do. Any cowboy knows how important it is to get back up on the horse after you've fallen off. If you got yourself a proper hat, you too could be a cowboy."

Eric had to chuckle, imagining himself as a cowboy. "Yeah, guess so."

Ichika whispered to Kaito, then smiled brightly at Kathy. "We would like to come too. We have to go home and resolve the working situation first. If management will not let us continue to work there as a couple then I will have to find another job and I do not know how long that will take. I will tell you and Taryn everything as it happens.

How do you say it? Keep your fingers crossed."

"We definitely will." Taryn said. "How about you Tadao? Will you come back next summer?"

"Yes, I would consider it. I had fun here, learned so many new things. I could practice the line dancing and be much better when we go to town. It will depend on work but I will try."

Kathy turned to Paige. "I bet it won't be hard to convince you. It has been so much fun watching you and Dustin connect. No doubt he'd be thrilled to have you back."

"He'd better be, or I'd give him what for!" humphed Paige.

Bobby came out from the kitchen just then to see how the meal was going. Taryn raised her coffee cup. "To the most incredible dude ranch chef ever." Everyone joined in and Bobby smiled broadly, winked at Taryn. "One love," he said before disappearing through the door again.

When breakfast was nearly over, Jesse walked to the table and thanked everyone for coming to the ranch.

"I just want to tell you all that this ranch has really come alive this past week. I can't imagine a group of people better matched for each other, and it's obvious you've become good friends. It's wonderful to see. You've all been a delight to serve." He glanced at Paige and Taryn. "And I want to extend a sincere thanks to these two ladies for putting together such a marvelous barbecue. With Bobby's help, they not only saved the day, they made it quite unique."

His remarks were met with a sincere round of applause.

A slow grin crossed his face. "And I'd like to let you all know that Taryn will be staying on for a while."

This brought cheers from most of the group, though Eric's seemed less enthusiastic.

"I know you've watched this week as we've grown close, and we want to see where our relationship will go. Thank you all for being supportive."

He walked to Taryn and gave her a warm kiss. She happily melted into him, then reluctantly pulled away and stood up.

"Can we talk for a minute, Jesse? I want to run some things by you about the possibility of setting up a yoga studio in that back room. Kathy mentioned last night that it might be a good amenity to offer your guests, and I think I'd like to do it while I'm here."

Jesse was delighted. "That sounds wonderful! Thank you, and Kathy, for that idea. Just let me know what you need; I'm happy to support you." He squinted in thought. "But I think it would be better if you used that empty tack room in the barn. It is heated, and it's bigger."

"No. The yoga room needs to be close to the massage rooms and the hot tub. We want a spa complex, so to speak. Anything in the barn would give off the wrong vibe."

Jesse relented. "You're right, of course. Makes sense. I'll go check out the back room, see if Larry's free to get it cleared out for you."

He walked off. Paige, who was standing nearby and had overheard the conversation, quickly rushed up to her friend.

"Taryn, that was amazing! Do you realize what you just did?"

Taryn knit her brows in consternation.

"You just stood your ground with Jesse. Remember what you told me about Wyatt helping Amy move, and how he contradicted you and you just let him? Well Jesse contradicted you and without even any hesitation you asserted your position. And he yielded."

A hint of pride crossed Taryn's face. "OMG, Paige. I did that without thinking. It was an automatic reaction, and I think it came from a place in me that has finally decided I know what I'm doing, that my opinions have value. And saying that, I'm now aware of how I really thought the opposite for so long." Her eyes widened in surprise.

"Yep, you got it girl," said Paige. "I can't tell you how wonderful it was to see you act like the strong, capable person you are instead of kow-towing to what some man wants. I watched that for far too long..."

"Felt really good, I can tell you," said Taryn. Reflectively, "I think I finally found my voice, finally feel like me."

Impulsively, both raised their hands for a high-five and laughed gleefully.

⌒

Taryn followed Paige back to her cabin to grab her bags. As soon as they walked in the door they fell into a long hug.

"Girl, what am I going to do in Seattle without you?" Paige wailed.

"Come on, it's only for two weeks, then you'll be back here," Taryn mock scolded.

"So what are you going to do about telling Amy and Josh about this new development? Aren't they expecting you to be around in a couple weeks for Josh's birthday?"

"I'm going to Zoom them this afternoon. After I figure out what to say to them. Right now I have no idea how I'm going to explain all this..."

Then she got quite somber.

"Paige, I'm scared. This is a huge step for me, way out of my comfort zone."

"I know it is, but be brave. I know Jesse is good for you, and you'll be fine." She patted Taryn's arm reassuringly. "And I'm only a phone call away."

"But what if Jesse gets tired of me? What if this whole thing was just one of those intense connections that was never supposed to last? There's a new bunch of people coming in to the ranch tonight. What if there's someone else he likes better? I don't know what I'd do ..."

"Cut it out. You're incredible, and Jesse knows it. He's not going to want someone else. He's so in love with you—it's written all over his face every time he looks at you."

"You think so?" Taryn asked hopefully.

"Girl, you know so. And you have to look at it from his side too. Remember that wall he had up till you got under his skin? He's really vulnerable now too, Taryn. He's fallen for a woman who lives in Seattle, has a whole life in Seattle, might very well decide she has to go back to Seattle. Which is fifteen hundred miles away from here. I bet he's even more scared than you are."

Taryn dropped her head. "I hadn't thought of that. You might be right."

"You guys are going to have to be very gentle with each other here."

Taryn laughed. "How is it you know so much about relationships all of a sudden? Especially since you're never really in one?"

"Just because I don't 'participate' doesn't mean I don't watch. I pay attention to all the rest of you. And movies. And books. Can't get away from seeing relationships actually."

"Well I'm glad you paid attention. That was good advice, and I'm going to take it. You are a treasure Paige."

"As are you my dear friend. Now help me get this stuff to the van. Dustin will yell at me if I'm late."

Jesse and Taryn stood arm in arm as they watched the vans being loaded with luggage and people. Dustin and Paige were off to the side, talking softly, with mournful eyes. One by one, each guest came up to thank Jesse, who expressed his appreciation in return.

"It has truly been wonderful having you all here. I sincerely hope you'll come again."

Kathy smiled. "I'm glad to hear you say that because we all may be back here next year."

"Really? I would ..." He glanced at Taryn. "I mean *we* would be thrilled to have the gang together again."

Taryn blushed, amazed that he would even for a minute be thinking they might still be a couple in a year. Quickly she hugged Kathy and promised to get in touch soon about exact dates.

Finally Paige left Dustin to say goodbye to Taryn.

Taryn hugged her friend close. "I am so going to miss you; thank God you're coming back in a couple weeks. What an adventure this week turned out to be!"

Paige opened the van door, then turned and gave Taryn a knowing smile.

"Well, girl. I'd say your adventure is just beginning."

Acknowledgments

There are many people to acknowledge for their contributions to this book.

My wonderful mother, Elneta, my sisters, Jackie and Janet, my friends Julia and Marsha, and husband, William, gave me such insightful feedback as my first readers. Thank you so much for your support. And thanks also to Kirsten Jensen for her thoughtful manuscript review.

I so appreciate Andrea Costantine for her continued guidance through the publishing process. Michael Kennedy, my editor, I cannot thank you enough for your honesty and direction during the editing journey. Victoria Wolf did a marvelous job with the cover design and layout.

To my dear sister Janet Hamilton, who painted the stunning picture for the cover, I send my deepest gratitude.

And, as always, I'm immensely grateful to my husband, William, who walks the path with me.